HARLEQUIN® *Presents*

Welcome to the October 2008 collection of Harlequin Presents!

This month read Sandra Marton's *The Sheikh's Defiant Bride*, the first book in her exciting trilogy THE SHEIKH TYCOONS. We also visit the Mediterranean, and two affluent heroes who aren't afraid to take what they want, in Julia James's *Greek Tycoon, Waitress Wife* and Robyn Donald's *His Majesty's Mistress*. Things begin to heat up at work (or should we say *after* work) for Abby in Anne Oliver's *Business in the Bedroom*. Maggie Cox also brings you a sexy office tale, this time involving an Italian tycoon and his unsuspecting personal assistant, in *Secretary Mistress, Convenient Wife*. Helen Bianchin weaves a story of attraction and convenience in *Purchased: His Perfect Wife,* in which cash-strapped Lara finds herself making a deal with her brooding stepbrother. Innocence is lost and passion abounds in *One Night with His Virgin Mistress* by Sara Craven, and housekeeper Liv's job description is more hands-on than most in *Housekeeper at His Beck and Call,* compliments of Susan Stephens.

We'd love to hear what you think about Harlequin Presents. E-mail us at Presents@hmb.co.uk, or join in the discussions at www.iheartpresents.com and www.sensationalromance.blogspot.com, where you'll also find more information about books and authors!

*Legally wed,
but he's never said,
"I love you."
They're...*

*The series where marriages are made
in haste...and love comes later.*

**Look out for more WEDLOCKED!
wedding stories available only from
Harlequin Presents®.**

Helen Bianchin

PURCHASED: HIS PERFECT WIFE

TORONTO • NEW YORK • LONDON
AMSTERDAM • PARIS • SYDNEY • HAMBURG
STOCKHOLM • ATHENS • TOKYO • MILAN • MADRID
PRAGUE • WARSAW • BUDAPEST • AUCKLAND

ISBN-13: 978-0-373-12763-4
ISBN-10:   0-373-12763-4

PURCHASED: HIS PERFECT WIFE

First North American Publication 2008.

www.eHarlequin.com

Printed in U.S.A.

All about the author...
Helen Bianchin

HELEN BIANCHIN grew up in New Zealand, an only child possessed by a vivid imagination and a love for reading. After four years of legal-secretarial work, Helen embarked on a working holiday in Australia, where she met her Italian-born husband, a tobacco share farmer in far north Queensland. His command of English was pitiful, and her command of Italian was nil. Fun? Oh yes! So too was being flung into cooking for workers immediately after marriage, stringing tobacco and living in primitive conditions.

It was a few years later that Helen, her husband and their daughter returned to New Zealand, settled in Auckland and added two sons to their family. Encouraged by friends to recount anecdotes of her years as a tobacco share farmer's wife living in an Italian community, Helen began setting words on paper, and her first novel was published in 1975.

Creating interesting characters and telling their stories remains as passionate a challenge for Helen as it did in the beginning of her writing career.

Spending time with family, reading and watching movies are high on Helen's list of pleasures. An animal lover, Helen says her Maltese terrier and two Birman cats regard her study as theirs as much as it is hers.

CHAPTER ONE

'Damn it.'

The despairing oath emerged as a barely audible condemnation as Lara checked her watch and cast the empty train-tracks a despairing glance.

The train was late. Not exactly a surprise, given the Sydney rail-system rarely kept to its timetable.

There was a general restlessness among the passengers lining the station platform, waiting to board.

An irritated feminine voice demanded querulously close by, 'Does anyone have any idea how inconvenient this delay is?'

Like you wouldn't believe, Lara answered silently.

'I have an important appointment!'

Oh my. As if you're the only one?

A bubble of hysterical laughter rose and died in her throat. Her own appointment was akin to life or death…figuratively, but almost equally as dire.

Help; the financial magnitude of it was hopeless.

Impossible, she perceived, unless a miracle occurred.

And she no longer believed in miracles. If she ever had. She spared the still-empty train tracks another anxious glance. Oh, *come on*, she silently begged, and barely refrained from uttering something incredibly unladylike.

Don't do this to me. Especially not today.

Silent prayers and unexpressed angst made not the slightest difference as the minutes ticked on, and she took a steadying breath and resigned herself to being late.

Alerting anyone to her delay wasn't going to happen, as she no longer possessed a mobile phone. She could access a phone booth, although the chances of finding one that actually worked in this particular station were minimal.

Several waiting passengers began to pace restlessly along the platform, their impatience matching her own, until collective sighs of relief heralded a train's arrival.

Lara boarded an overloaded carriage and was forced to stand. Worse, as the train cleared the station, it met torrential rain slanting down in wind-driven sheets that didn't show signs of ceasing any time soon.

Great. She hadn't brought an umbrella.

A sign the day…and the power of the Deity…wasn't done with her?

Somehow it seemed appropriate, given she was due— make that *overdue*—for an appointment with a prestigious firm of lawyers in order to be apprised of the contents of two wills, as a result of the tragic accidental death of her mother and stepfather in France.

Emotion welled up inside, and she willed herself not to cry. The shedding of tears in public wasn't going to happen.

Caring, affectionate Darius Alexander had provided the happiness sorely missing in her mother's first marriage, accepting and treating Lara as if she'd been his own.

Not so his son Wolfe, who ten years ago had viewed Suzanne and her seventeen-year-old daughter Lara predominantly as fortune-hunters planning to live the high life at his father's expense.

Something so not true it was pathetic, given Suzanne had insisted on signing a pre-nup prior to her marriage to Darius. A fact Wolfe would be forced to accept when the contents of both Darius and Suzanne's wills were revealed. Together with the addendum, citing Lara's welfare was Suzanne's financial responsibility.

Within a year of the marriage Wolfe had declined Darius' offer to join his conglomerate's directorial board and had taken up a lucrative offer in New York, choosing instead to forge his own path in the business arena.

Lara had completed her studies, qualified as a chef, and spent time in France and Italy for a few years, honing her skills before returning to Sydney.

Two years ago she'd formed a business partnership with Paul Evans, sunk all her savings into a restaurant in a trendy suburb, and had worked long hours to make it a success.

Something she'd achieved, providing fine food at reasonable prices for a steadily increasing clientele.

Life had been good…until Paul had fled the country after clearing out their business bank account, and her own, because she'd foolishly trusted him.

Not coincidentally, the theft had been timed to occur the day after Darius and Suzanne had embarked on a lengthy European tour, ensuring lack of hands-on parental support. The police were called in, lawyers consulted, charges laid, but the wheels of justice had moved slowly.

Pride had ensured the resultant mess was *her* problem, and in an effort to conserve funds she'd given up her leased apartment and downsized to lodgings, sold her car and resorted to public transport.

However, the financial damage had been acute, and minimizing staff by personally working long shifts had done little to ease the situation. Bank assistance was withdrawn, and she'd dealt with lack of funds as best she could with a short term high-interest loan from a less than desirable source.

A man who'd spelt out terms in cold hard facts.

Pay on time, and everything will be fine.

Followed by a succinct and frightening, *don't...and it won't*.

The implications had been vividly clear, and only a fool would have failed to recognize them.

Borrowing money in such circumstances had not been a wise move, she reflected grimly. The reality of missing a payment had provided a vivid reminder of just who she was dealing with.

Not a bank-loan officer trained to provide a psychologically couched response with seeming regret.

Instead, a ruthless man who dealt with desperate people who were denied access to normal lending-institutions and who accepted the terms, aware of the risks.

Something he'd revealed in chilling detail, elaborating precisely on what she could expect if she failed to pay on time.

Apprehension didn't begin to cover it.

All-consuming fear barely came close.

She'd been barely able to function. She'd rarely eaten, and she hadn't been able to sleep.

At which point she'd put aside pride and appealed for Darius' help, verbally given without hesitation. He would, he'd assured, attend to it as soon as he accessed a fax machine.

Lara's relief had been short-lived. Reduced to mere hours, before she'd been alerted that a road accident had claimed both her mother's and stepfather's lives.

It was Wolfe who'd relayed the shattering news, taken immediate control, flying from New York to France to attend to formalities before jetting in to Sydney, then conferring with her over arrangements and providing support at the funeral service.

Days during which she'd functioned on auto-pilot and lost track of time as she hid her grief in public and succumbed to it in private.

Tracking down her biological father had resulted in a curt dismissal at being involved in any way.

Lara recalled a host of kaleidoscopic memories...an alcoholic father whose rages had been volatile and many, the bitter arguments and physical abuse her mother had endeavoured to shield from her daughter; the day Marc Sommers had beaten Lara, Suzanne had gathered a few clothes into a suitcase, taken hold of Lara's hand and fled to another city in another State.

There was no difficulty in picturing their rented two-room flat, the long hours Suzanne had worked, or the school Lara had attended in a less than salubrious inner-city suburb.

Tough beginnings, which Suzanne had toiled hard to change…and succeeded, gradually carving a better life for them both, enhanced by Suzanne's chance meeting with Darius, his persistent courtship and their marriage.

The subtle change in train speed brought Lara back to the present, and she stifled a grateful sigh as she alighted at the inner-city station.

Several minutes later she took the escalator and reached street level, only to dash to the intersection to catch the lights at a nearby traffic-controlled pedestrian crossing.

Rain pelted down. She stepped into a huge rain puddle, which sent water splashing fountain-like over her black trousers. By the time she reached the opposite pavement she felt, and probably looked, like a drowned cat.

Could the day get any worse?

Don't even *think* about it, a mischievous imp taunted silently, whereupon Lara promptly banished it elsewhere. The address housing Darius' prestigious firm of lawyers was two blocks away, and she dodged the rain and fellow pedestrians at a fast pace, entered the marble-tiled foyer, then paused a few moments to extract a handkerchief to dry off her hair.

A wasted effort, which she discarded with a sense of hopeless fatalism as she crossed to the bank of lifts, pressed the arrowed 'up' button and stood waiting for any one of several electronic cubicles to descend to ground level.

The melodic ping announcing the arrival of a lift caught her attention, and she rode it with some trepidation to the designated floor.

Any minute soon she'd face her inimitable stepbrother.

In his late thirties, Wolfe Alexander's interest was purported to focus as much on women as it did on business. With immense success in both areas, according to Darius, who'd begun to despair of his son marrying and providing an heir…or returning to Sydney to take up a rightful position on the board of directors.

Darius' son…a man who was a force to be reckoned with on every level. As he'd proven with an incident during her eighteenth birthday party which Lara had chosen to obliterate from her memory…and thought she had, until she'd stood silently at Wolfe's side two days ago at the formal burial of his father and her mother.

The lift slid to a smooth halt and Lara emerged into the open foyer, where Darius' legal firm occupied the entire floor, hosting an imposing reception area with an equally soignée receptionist who could, Lara perceived with unaccustomed cynicism, moonlight as a model…and possibly did.

Exceedingly damp and bedraggled wasn't a good look, Lara conceded as she identified herself, apologized for her lateness…and requested direction to the bathroom.

What did another few minutes matter?

'Of course.' The receptionist rose to her feet and extended a hand. 'Would you like me to take care of your coat?'

'Thanks.'

It didn't take long to sweep the wet length of her blonde hair into a loose knot, secure it with a large hinged clip, touch colour to her lips and smooth her black top.

A deep calming breath, and she returned to Reception where an assistant led her to a spacious executive office, announced and ushered her in, then closed the door behind her.

Two men rose to their feet, and Lara acknowledged the lawyer, offered an apology, then turned slightly towards the tall, broad-shouldered, impeccably tailored figure silhouetted against floor-to-ceiling glass, met a pair of dark, enigmatic grey eyes, and inclined her head. 'Wolfe.'

It was impossible to tell anything from his expression, and she didn't even try.

'Lara.' His voice was a smooth, slightly accented drawl, and she endeavoured to control the nervous tension he managed to arouse without any seeming effort at all.

There was something vaguely primitive apparent, an electric, almost raw sexuality that was dangerous to any woman's peace of mind...especially *hers*.

Dear God. How could she ever forget the first time she'd met him mere weeks before the advent of Suzanne's marriage to Darius?

One look...and she'd melted into an ignominious puddle, aware of every breath, and unable to voice a sensible sentence in his presence.

The image of a high-school jock who held every grade-twelve female student in lascivious thrall had ceased to exist...replaced in a heartbeat by a twenty-seven-year-old tall, dark and ruggedly attractive male whom Lara had elevated to godlike status.

In response, Wolfe had been polite but distant and coolly tolerant whenever they happened to be in the same place at the same time...which hadn't been too often.

Lara's eighteenth birthday had been something special... a beautiful gown, friends, music...and Wolfe. She'd felt incredibly grown up. Mature. A flute of champagne on an empty stomach, followed later by another, had provided her with the courage to turn a fleeting, solitary kiss to her cheek from Wolfe into something else as she'd turned her head and met his lips with her own. Emboldened, she'd lifted her arms and linked her hands together at his nape, pressed in against him, opened her mouth and sought his tongue with her own.

She felt his initial hesitation, followed by the involuntary sweep of his tongue against her own…then he slowly lifted his head and gently put her at arm's length.

His quietly voiced, 'Meet me later,' sent her heart soaring, and she was hardly able to wait until the evening came to an end.

He was going to take her in his arms and kiss her again… *really* kiss her. And it would be everything she'd imagined, and more.

Every nerve-end throbbed into awareness, and she became supremely conscious of every breath she took…its jagged quality as she failed to control the excitement flooding her veins.

Dimmed lights provided the grounds with a shadowed illumination as he led her beneath the spreading branches of a magnificent jacaranda tree.

It was there Wolfe drew her into his arms and brushed his mouth to her own, deepening the kiss as she sighed and sought the play of taut muscle and sinew beneath his cotton shirt.

Pleasure, sweet and evocative, took hold of her vulnerable emotions and captured them. She couldn't think…and knew she didn't want to…as his tongue met her own, traced its outline, then began a sensual exploration that promised heat and passion. Everything she'd dreamed a kiss could be.

Her lower body arched involuntarily against his own. Seconds later the breath hitched in her throat as he plundered at will.

Oh my God.

The earth moved…she was willing to swear on it, and she lost all sensation of time and place, for there was only the man and the intense sexual awareness he aroused.

She didn't want it to end, and a faint protest escaped her lips as he lifted his head, and her eyes widened into huge, dark pools as he put her at arm's length.

Dear heaven, *please*, she silently begged in a desperate need to feel the warmth of his mouth on her own. The heat, the intense emotion he managed to arouse without any seeming effort at all.

Had she said the words out loud?

She didn't know as Wolfe grasped hold of her chin and lifted it high.

'Very pleasant. But…just for the record…I have no intention of following Darius' example by becoming involved with his second wife's daughter.'

Harsh, angry words that tore her vulnerable heart apart and left it raw and bleeding.

Didn't he know he'd succeeded in branding her his own with that erotically evocative kiss?

She felt cold, so cold her body shook with it.

How could he?

It was pride and pride alone that wrought her response. It cost dearly to summon cynicism, but she managed it…just. 'So, what was that we just shared? A lesson in futility?'

His eyes were dark, slumbrous in the moonlit night.

'Yes, damn you.'

Humiliated beyond measure, she turned and walked away from him, uncaring whether he followed her or not. And indoors she met Darius, momentarily paused, saw his eyes sharpen at her obvious distress, then she gave a choked cry and ran quickly upstairs to her room, removed her clothes, took a leisurely shower…and wept until there were no tears left.

'Please. Sit down.'

The words brought Lara slamming back to the present, and for a brief second her eyes widened as Wolfe indicated the leather-buttoned chair close to his own.

How long had she been locked in the past? Dear heaven, hopefully only a number of fleeting seconds. *Years* had passed since her eighteenth birthday…ten, to be precise…and she was no longer a sexually vulnerable teenager, prey to burgeoning emotions.

Lara chose the chair furthest away from Wolfe, unsure whether it was a minor act of defiance or the need to put some distance between them.

The lawyer crossed behind his desk, collected a file and opened it as he sank into his chair.

There was a discreet knock on the door, and an assistant entered with a tray containing a steaming pot of tea and coffee together with the requisite cups, saucers, milk and sugar.

The norm? Preferential treatment for important clientele, or an offering in preparation for unexpected news?

Whatever…she held the hope it wouldn't involve too much time, for she was due to begin the afternoon shift a few hours from now.

Lara took her tea strong, and she endeavoured to still a slight shaky feeling as she sipped the brew and waited for the lawyer to begin.

Legalese tended to be long-winded as various clauses sought to cover every contingency. Darius' will cited numerous issues, bequeathing Suzanne the use of their principal residence and a generous income from certain allocated personal assets…such assets to be held in trust for his only son, Wolfe Ignatius Alexander.

The remainder of his personal estate was to be held in trust and released to Wolfe upon the event of Wolfe's marriage and the issue of children.

Darius' business assets, comprising the Alexander Conglomerate and its various companies…bequeathed to Wolfe and Lara in equal shares.

Lara opened her mouth in disbelief, then closed it again as the lawyer continued.

Wolfe's fifty-per-cent share conditional in the event he relocated to Sydney and took control as head of the directorial board. If this was not met within three months of Darius' demise, Wolfe's share of the Alexander Conglomerate and its various companies would be sold and the proceeds donated to several nominated charities.

Lara's fifty-per-cent share to be held in trust for her children, with Lara receiving dividend income from those shares.

Suzanne's insistence on a pre-nuptial agreement that allowed her the use of one residence together with an annuity should Darius predecease her was something Lara had known about for several years.

If Wolfe was surprised by the existence of a pre-nup at Suzanne's instigation, he gave no evidence of it as the lawyer condensed the contents of Suzanne's will.

Personal effects, items of jewellery and any cash held in Suzanne's bank accounts went to her only daughter, Lara Anne Sommers, together with Suzanne's annuity in perpetuity to Lara, the use of Suzanne's principal residence to pass to Lara during her lifetime, with any remaining assets to be held in trust for Lara's children.

Darius had been a generous benefactor, gifting Suzanne an enviable lifestyle, comprising frequent travel, a more-than-generous allowance and numerous gifts of jewellery, ensuring Suzanne had wanted for nothing.

The implications sank in with stark reality.

Darius had played his last card.

Attempting to achieve in death what he'd been unable to achieve during his lifetime…by organizing his affairs to have his only son return to Sydney and take control of his business interests.

'I respectfully suggest your decision regarding the Alexander Conglomerate is paramount,' the lawyer posed, and Wolfe inclined his head in agreement.

There followed a rundown of Darius' personal and business

assets, together with those of Suzanne…untouchable until both estates went to probate, which could, given the complexity of assets, take several months.

Lara rose to her feet as the consultation came to an end, and walked at Wolfe's side to Reception, collected her coat and crossed to the bank of lifts.

There were numerous issues regarding Suzanne's personal effects, but for the life of her she couldn't think of them now.

The lift arrived and she entered it and stood in silence at Wolfe's side as it descended swiftly to ground level.

In such small confines, his height and breadth of shoulder made her increasingly aware of her petite stature.

The contrast between them was marked. Wolfe's dark hair, sculptured bone structure and dark, slate-grey eyes owed much to his late mother's European ancestry. Whereas Lara possessed ash-blonde hair, fine-boned features and brilliant sapphire-blue eyes…the antithesis of his own.

The lift reached ground level, and they walked out onto the pavement to witness the rain replaced by weak sunshine.

Lara paused hesitantly as concern vied with the stark reality of what she could possibly arrange regarding her outstanding debt to the ominously threatening loan shark.

There was a palatial home she could live in upon probate… but not sell or rent out. A generous annuity in perpetuity paid into her bank account each month upon probate. Shares worth a small fortune…to be held in trust and not sold, from which she'd derive a very sizable income…again, upon probate. Suzanne's jewellery and personal effects which she'd choose to treasure and never sell. A restaurant she'd have to walk away from any day soon if serious financial help wasn't forthcoming.

Assets, none of which were liquid…ensuring she was asset rich, but cash poor. With no hope in hell of raising the large amount of cash needed by midnight to pay off the loan shark.

Even if she presented copies of Darius' and Suzanne's wills, no bank would come to her aid with such a large amount within hours.

Could she…dared she…approach Wolfe, explain her predicament and request his financial assistance?

Ice entered her veins and chilled her body.

There was no other way.

None.

So what did she have to lose…except her pride?

CHAPTER TWO

'CAN we talk?' Stark, minimum words that cost her dearly, and incurred a probing look.

'There's something you want to discuss?'

His voice was a faintly inflected drawl, and she suppressed an involuntary shiver.

Lara spared him a quick glance and gleaned little from his expression. Assertiveness was the key. 'Yes.'

'In that case, let's do so over lunch.'

Share a meal with him? She really didn't want to spend any more time than necessary… Time was something she didn't have!

He sensed her hesitation, and his eyes narrowed slightly. She looked too slender, her features too pale, and she resembled a cat on hot bricks.

Grief, without doubt, had to be taken into account…but why did he have the feeling it was more than that? A broken romance? There had been no boyfriend evident to lend support during the funeral service, nor to attend the gathering afterwards.

He told himself he didn't care…and knew it to be untrue. For, despite the intervening years, he still retained a vivid recall of her teenage crush, and the method with which he'd dealt with it. The surprising sweetness of her young mouth;

her reaction to his touch; the way she'd felt in his arms, and her uninhibited response.

It had affected him more than he'd imagined possible, and left him with a lingering sense of frustration in the knowledge he could have taken her. What had held him back? Remorse? Guilt? At the time he'd refused to contemplate it might be anything else…and he'd grasped opportunity with both hands soon after by relocating to New York, where he'd focused on forging his own fortune.

During the following years he'd met up with Darius in various parts of the world, and during infrequent appearances in Sydney, where he preferred hotel accommodation to staying as a guest in his father's home. Dinner invitations that had included Lara…who'd stoically refused to ignore him, yet had treated him with such incredible politeness it had made him want to shake her.

Not unlike the feeling he entertained now.

'We both need to eat,' Wolfe ventured silkily.

Did she have a choice?

'A sandwich and coffee,' she conceded, aware it was all she could afford.

'When was the last time you ate a decent meal?'

The question came out of left field, and she stiffened at the underlying censure. 'In case you've forgotten, I spend my time in a kitchen cooking professionally for a living.'

'For clientele.'

'The nature of the business,' she responded, and incurred his dark gaze.

'An hour or two enjoying a leisurely meal in my company is abhorrent to you?'

Difficult. Unnerving. But not abhorrent. She closed her eyes, then opened them again. 'Of course not.'

They were walking along a busy city-street, and she hesitated as Wolfe indicated a restaurant she knew to be ruin-ously expensive.

'Relax.'

Sure. Like she could do that!

The maître d' took one look at Wolfe, determined an aura of wealth, and ushered them to a well-positioned table.

Within minutes the drinks waiter elicited their order, and Lara opted to stay with chilled water, as did Wolfe.

The menu offered a superb variety, and she perused the se-lection with care.

'Do you have a preference?'

Oh God, she didn't want to do this!

'I'm not very hungry.'

Wolfe cast her a brief glance over the top of the menu, then went ahead and ordered bruschetta, two entrées, two mains and intimated dessert could wait until later.

She opened her mouth to protest, only to close it again as she incurred his dark, unyielding look.

'You really want to argue?'

Give it up, a silent voice warned.

The temptation to launch into her request was uppermost, if only to get it out there and be done with it—for the thought of playing polite and conducting a meaningless conversation almost brought her undone.

He looked every inch the man he'd become. Hardened, ruthless, powerful. Someone it would be wise not to toy with…unless you were prepared to face the consequences.

Successful beyond measure, Darius had been known to reveal with pride, with an apartment overlooking New York's Central Park, residences in London and the south of France, to name a few.

While she was almost destitute and in debt up to her eyeballs.

Some comparison!

Did—*could*—Wolfe know of her financial circumstances?

Probably not. Unless he'd made it his business to find out. Despite privacy laws, information wasn't too difficult to elicit if one knew how to circumvent conventional channels.

The mere thought sickened her, and she felt a slight degree of relief as a waiter appeared and placed a platter onto the table.

The bruschetta was tempting, although, given the state of her nerves, forking morsels of food into her mouth would require concentrated effort.

'Eat, Lara.'

To refuse would be churlish, given a banana followed by coffee had comprised breakfast, and anything she managed to consume this evening would be eaten on the run. If nothing else, she needed food for sustenance and energy to maintain long working hours.

'How long do you intend to stay in Sydney?'

He met her gaze and held it. 'As long as it takes.'

An ambiguous answer that didn't commit him to anything.

Would he comply with the conditions of Darius' will?

It really was no concern of hers whether he did or not.

Lara moved the food around on her plate, and was so caught up with nerves she didn't trust herself to lift her fork.

'You wanted to run something by me?' Wolfe prompted, and caught her sudden look of anguish.

This was hard, but she couldn't prevaricate, wouldn't pretend. Only explain…and ask.

Which she did, as briefly as possible, whilst outlining only the pertinent facts and her desperate urgency for funds.

The spectre of the loan shark hovered over her like the sword of Damocles, ever threatening, and poised to fall any time soon. Fear consumed her, stretching her nerves to breaking point.

There was nothing to be gleaned from his expression, making it impossible to discern whether he'd view her request favourably or not.

'What amount do you have in mind?'

She mentioned a sum, and he didn't even blink.

'You perceive it as a gift?'

'*No.*' Genuine shock widened her eyes, and her hands shook slightly as she replaced her water goblet down onto the table. 'A loan.' She closed her eyes, then opened them again. 'Using the shares bequeathed me under the terms of Darius' will as collateral.'

She'd done the maths, had agonized and lost sleep over the figures, minimizing them to bare essentials in order to clear accumulated debts and purchase a vehicle. 'I'll pay you back every cent, with interest.'

'Over what time frame?'

Lara relayed an estimation. 'Less,' she assured him quickly. 'I can utilize the annuity from Suzanne's estate and transfer it directly to you.'

Wolfe surveyed her carefully, then offered a silky negative. 'No.'

Her features paled, and her eyes became large stricken pools. She had nowhere to go…no one else she could ask.

Loan sharks lent money on a strictly short-term basis, and non-payment wrought dire consequences.

She could feel the germ of anger begin to seed and take hold, sparking into flames that owed much to the past.

Uppermost was the desire to pick up the salt-shaker and hurl it at him. She consciously placed her hands onto her lap in an effort at control.

Any hope Wolfe might honour Darius' verbal assurance of financial help died a natural death, and she rose to her feet, unable to bear so much as another minute in his company. 'Go back to New York and have a nice life.'

'Sit down.' Dark slate-grey eyes seared hers. 'I'm not done.'

'*I* am!'

Lara turned away from the table, and in the next instant a

hand closed over her wrist, manacling her as securely as steel restraints.

'Let me go.' The words husked from her throat in a low growl, and her eyes flared with brilliant sapphire chips.

This close, she was supremely conscious of his height and breadth of shoulder, the clean, laundered smell of his clothes and the faint, teasing aroma of his cologne.

'Sit down…please.'

The 'please' did little to appease her anger as she glared at him. 'Give me one reason why I should.'

His gaze didn't waver, and a muscle bunched at the edge of his jaw. 'I have a suggestion.' One he had no hesitation in making…having reached the decision with split-second decisiveness.

Lara stilled, and her glare became tinged with wariness. 'I'm not sure I want to hear it.'

She was hardly aware of being manoeuvered down into her seat until Wolfe released her wrist and resumed his position opposite.

'I'll settle your debts.'

The wariness increased. 'You just gave me a categorical *no*.'

'To providing you with a loan,' Wolfe corrected, adding, 'Or accepting a transfer of Suzanne's annuity.'

Why did she suddenly have this icy chill feathering the length of her spine?

'As it stands, the future of the Alexander Conglomerate is at risk. Your bequeathed half-share is projected into the next generation via issue of your children. While mine, should I not relocate to Sydney and assume directorship, will disappear entirely.' His gaze seared her own. 'Not something, I think you'll agree, Darius intended for his billion-dollar conglomerate?'

She knew Darius had accumulated immense wealth…but *that* much?

Only a fool would allow an investment of that size to slip through their fingers. And Wolfe was no fool.

'So you'll base yourself in Sydney.' It wasn't a question, but a statement of fact.

'I'll honour my father's wishes,' he informed her silkily, pausing as the waiter removed their plates and intimated their main course would soon be served. 'A stable consolidation is essential for the future of the conglomerate, don't you agree?'

There could be only one answer. 'Yes.'

He was playing a delicate game, one that required verbal skill and the power of persuasion. Something he was particularly noted for in the business arena, together with his ruthless ability to win against incredible odds.

Darius' will had set out a deliberate plan in an attempt to achieve in death what he hadn't been able to bring to fruition during his lifetime.

Wolfe observed Lara's expressive features, divining the wariness evident, the faint curiosity…and closed in for the kill.

'I'll ensure the funds you require are transferred into your bank account within twenty-four hours.'

Her relief was palpable as the horrendous weight of her liability to the loan shark was seen to disappear, and her voice shook a little.

'Thank you.'

'Together with an equal amount to ensure any outstanding bills are paid, any temporary reduction in your staff's wages are reimbursed.'

The waiter delivered their main course, and she didn't speak until he was out of earshot.

'You're being unbelievably generous.' An instinctive wariness began to unfold, together with suspicion.

'I'll clear the restaurant mortgage-debt, and cover all necessary refurbishment.'

There had to be a catch. A price she'd have to pay.

How many possibilities were there? Too few, she acknowledged silently, and in reality, only one.

Yet she had to ask. 'In return for what?'

One dark eyebrow slanted, and his voice held an edge of mockery. 'Occupying my home, my bed.'

Her eyes blazed blue fire. 'As your mistress?'

'No.'

He sounded mildly amused, and at that moment she truly hated him.

'Then...*what*?' Lara demanded.

'My wife.'

CHAPTER THREE

For a moment Lara lost the power of speech, and she felt the blood drain from her cheeks.

'If this is a joke,' she began shakily, 'it's in very bad taste.'

Wolfe observed her in silence, noting the way her eyes dilated and became dark, her slightly parted mouth as she unconsciously held her breath.

'You can't be serious?' she managed at last. The concept was ludicrous. Beyond belief. *Impossible.*

'Very serious,' Wolfe assured her solemnly.

'Why?' It was a strangled, heart-wrenching cry from the depths of her soul.

'Children.'

It took a few seconds for her to get it, and even then Wolfe chose to spell it out.

'Our equal shares in the Alexander Conglomerate are consigned in trust to the issue of children from your marriage, and from my own. Something which will create complex difficulties, and ultimately cause the conglomerate to disintegrate in the next generation.' He waited a beat as his gaze speared her own. 'It won't happen if you and I wed each other and the children stipulated in Darius' will issue from our marriage.'

'You're offering me a business deal that will tie up a few

loose ends and keep everything in the family?' Lara deduced with deceptive quietness.

'Does that bother you?'

The thought of being a 'loose end' didn't sit well.

'*Yes*, damn it!' She took a deep breath, then let it out slowly. Aiming for cool, calm and collected was proving difficult when there was an internal battle going on. 'You're proposing a *convenient* marriage?' She was on a roll. 'Which will entail…?'

'Sharing a home, a partnership in bed and out of it. A generous allowance.' He lifted a shoulder in a negligible shrug. 'An enviable lifestyle. Children, eventually, God willing.' He paused fractionally. 'Is that sufficiently specific?'

He was still. Too still, like a predator indolently waiting to pounce.

'And, if I refuse, you'll withdraw your offer to transfer funds.' Her voice shook with the effort it cost her to speak.

'Yes.'

She picked up her water goblet, and barely restrained the urge to throw the contents in his face.

For a few timeless seconds her eyes blazed with anger as they collided with his, and it took all her control to restore the goblet onto the table.

'A wife, bought and paid for.'

His expression hardened a little at her succinct summation, and his grey eyes assumed the colour of dark slate.

A silent war rose to the fore, and she battled against the unbearable need to hit him.

It didn't help that he knew.

'Don't discount the offer, Lara,' Wolfe warned with dangerous silkiness. 'You have no other option.'

Wasn't that the truth! Yet the fact rankled unbearably.

'You expect me to meekly comply?'

Meek and Lara didn't feature on the same page, he mused idly. The smitten teenager of ten years ago had grown in spirit and attitude to become the fiercely independent young woman seated opposite him today. Who, despite being down and almost out, could still attempt to do battle with him.

Wolfe leaned back in his chair. 'The choice is yours.'

Some choice.

A deal with the Devil…or the Devil to pay.

It was no contest.

'If…*if* I agree,' she continued in a voice stiff with latent anger, 'When do you envisage the marriage to take place?'

'As soon as it can be arranged, by special licence.'

That soon.

'Provide me with all the relevant paperwork involving your debts, and I'll take care of them.'

'When?' It sounded so *mercenary*, but she was past caring.

'The funds you so urgently need will be available in your bank tomorrow. The balance authorized immediately after our signatures appear on the marriage certificate.'

This is *business*, she reminded herself bitterly, with no sentiment or trust where money was involved.

However, it rankled…badly. Her chin lifted a little and her eyes assumed a deep sapphire-blue.

'I want to continue running my restaurant.' It was her pride and joy…more. And she refused to give it up.

Wolfe's expression hardened. 'You can retain the restaurant as an investment,' he allowed equably. 'But your continued involvement will be minimal.'

She suddenly had trouble regulating her breathing. 'Excuse me?'

'You heard.'

No quarter given in those obdurate words, and she barely resisted the temptation to tell him exactly what he could do with his proposal.

Think, a tiny voice prompted in silent warning.

She had everything to lose if she walked away from him.

What price pride in the face of wisdom?

Besides, marriage didn't have to mean for ever.

If she gave him an heir…

Yet how could she walk away from her own child?

The whole scenario was fraught.

'You can't expect me to give you an answer now?'

'Tonight.'

'I'm due at work.' She spared a glance at her watch, and stood to her feet. 'Oh hell, *now*.' Staff were at a minimum, and she could ill afford to be late. 'I finish somewhere between eleven and midnight.'

Wolfe signalled the waiter, extracted his wallet and paid the bill. 'I'll drive you.'

She was walking quickly. 'I can take a train.'

'But you won't.'

What was the point in arguing? A car would reach her destination more quickly than public transport.

Minutes later he disabled the locking mechanism of a top-of-the-range black Lexus, saw her seated, then he slid in behind the wheel and eased the car into the stream of traffic.

The Rocks area held numerous cafés and restaurants, and Lara directed him to double-park outside her own.

Wolfe handed her a card with his mobile-phone number. 'I'll expect your call.'

She slipped it into her purse, inclined her head, then sped quickly down a side alley to the back entrance, and used her key in the lock.

In the small back-room space she discarded her outer clothes, donned her chef's uniform, tied on an apron, wound the length of her hair beneath a protective cap…and went to work.

They were one staff member down, which made for chaos in the kitchen, with delays and short tempers as three pairs of hands attempted to do the work of four.

Shontelle acted as maître d', taking reservations, welcoming patrons, ensuring they were seated.

Sally held the position of head waitress, and both girls had been with Lara's from the day the restaurant had opened. Long-time friends who were equally as dedicated to the success of the restaurant as Lara herself.

Together they'd enjoyed the good times, and had stayed on to help Lara battle through the financial mess left by her business partner.

Around ten the rush began to ease as customers lingered over dessert and coffee, and by eleven the numbers had dwindled down to a few.

It was a relief when the last patrons left, the doors closed, the kitchen staff finished up, and all that remained was the nightly cleaning. Something which didn't take long as Sally lifted chairs onto tables while Lara vacuumed the floors.

There hadn't been time to give Wolfe's suggestion much thought, except in fleeting moments which in no way encompassed the big picture of marriage, children…intimacy.

How was she going to deal with *that*?

Being so aware of the man, his sensual chemistry and the way it affected her. His sexual partner…and knowing, to him, it would just be *sex*.

That love didn't enter the equation, and never would.

Could she live with him and pretend?

Lara moved the vacuum cleaner with increased speed in an attempt to expend some nervous energy.

For heaven's sake!

Wolfe was offering a way out.

What other option did she have?

Disappear and assume another identity? Contact the police and report the loan shark for harassment?

Sure…like either of those scenarios would work!

Besides, it wasn't part of her nature to run from anything.

Marry a billionaire, enjoy an enviable lifestyle, and bear him a child or two.

A hundred…oh, why not go for broke and make it a *thousand*…women would jump at the chance.

So what was the big deal?

Just a little matter of emotional engagement…*hers*.

Wolfe Alexander affected her like no other man she'd met. At seventeen, she had melted at the initial moment of introduction, almost frighteningly aware of the degree of raw sexuality he exuded. A teenage crush that had lingered long and almost brought her undone.

She'd moved on, matured, indulged in a brief relationship or two…but there was no one who'd come close to Wolfe, or the emotions he roused.

'That's it, we're done.'

The sound of Sally's voice brought Lara back to the present, and she switched off the vacuum cleaner, stowed it in the cupboard, then changed into her outdoor clothes.

'I need to make a phone call.'

She had three choices: use the phone here, a phone booth, or the phone in the hallway at her boarding house.

'I'll plug in some music and wait,' Sally directed, removing her earphones.

They had a steadfast rule—no female staff left alone this late at night.

'I won't be long.' Lara extracted Wolfe's card and crossed to the phone, all too aware the nerves in her stomach had twisted into a painful knot.

Seconds later she cursed beneath her breath as she keyed in a wrong digit and had to start over.

Wolfe answered on the third ring, intoning, 'Alexander,' in a voice that sounded deep and slightly more accented over the phone.

'Lara.' She identified herself at once.

'You've reached a decision?'

It was hardly the time or the occasion for small talk, and she didn't even try. 'Yes.'

'And?'

Heaven help her. She gripped the handset a little tighter. 'Yes.'

Lara wasn't sure how she expected him to respond.

'I'll be in touch tomorrow with relevant details.' There was a click and the line went dead.

It took a second or three for her to realize he'd cut the connection, and her fingers tightened momentarily before she replaced the handset.

He at least could have acknowledged her acceptance!

Oh, get real, a silent voice chastised. *What did you expect?* Forget sentiment…there was none.

So what did she care?

Even thinking about Wolfe in the role of husband accelerated her pulse and did strange things to her equilibrium.

Oh, for heaven's sake…get over it! He's just a man, like any other… And she knew she lied.

Ten years down the track she still retained a vivid recollection of his erotic kiss… Worse, the oral foreplay he'd metered out as a stark warning, and the way it had affected her.

What would he be like as a lover?

Don't go there. At least not now, not yet.

For, if she allowed herself to go down that path, she'd never make it to the wedding.

Best not to think too deeply…and keep busy!

It was time to check the windows, external doors, set the alarm, lock up, then pull down the security grill and padlock it.

A nightly routine they executed in tandem before walking briskly to the nearest train station.

Lara took a deep breath, turned and collected her bag, then she signalled Sally she was ready to leave.

It wasn't until they'd boarded the train that she remembered a vital phone call she should have made to the loan shark, begging a further twenty-four-hour extension, and the promise payment of the total funds would be made in cash.

Something twisted painfully in the region of her stomach as she checked the time, and her heart began to pound.

The week's loan extension ran out at midnight.

She needed to make that call…fast. Explain, give Wolfe's name as verification the money would be paid.

Please hurry, she bade silently as the train sped towards their station, and as they disembarked she had to restrain herself from running to the boarding house.

The inner-city suburb of Darlinghurst contained some less-than-salubrious streets where numerous bedsits and boarding houses existed in old converted homes. The dark of night and dim street-lighting hid their daytime grime and general state of disrepair.

Definitely not an area in which to linger long, and as far removed from Lara's former apartment as chalk from cheese.

Lara's relief was palpable as she entered the house via the front entrance, and she extracted the requisite coins from her purse to feed the pay-phone.

Seconds later the phone rang out, and she redialled, hoping, praying, for an answer. But there was none, and a second later a male figure appeared out of nowhere, a hard hand angled beneath her jaw, and she was lifted off her feet, then slammed against the wall.

Fear, stark and terrifying, almost made her pass out as the man's face came within inches of her own.

'Pay up by midnight tomorrow. Or else.' His grip tightened. 'Blink if you've got the message.'

Lara instantly obeyed, almost choking beneath his relentless grip, then he released her and disappeared out the front entrance as she subsided to the floor in a state of shock.

'Hey. You OK?'

She looked up in dazed terror, recognized a male tenant, and tried to speak…except no sound came out.

'You need help?'

Like you wouldn't believe!

'Want me to call someone?'

There was only one person who could handle this mess, and Lara reached into her purse, withdrew Wolfe's card and indicated the mobile-phone number written on the back.

She was dimly aware of a brief one-sided conversation, then the tenant led her into her room, sat her down and applied a dampened towel to her throat.

Lara had little recollection of how long it took Wolfe to appear…only that suddenly he was there, looming large in the small room, his features grim as he took in her pale features, the darkness apparent in her eyes.

He didn't say a word as he took the few steps necessary to reach her, and her gaze never left his as he hunkered down in front of her.

With care he removed the damp towel, and a muscle bunched in one cheek as he saw the reddened marks apparent, noted the pain it caused her to swallow, and trailed gentle fingers along the underside of her jaw. He was close, too close, she registered…and she hated that he appeared to swamp her.

She was aware of him thanking her rescuer, then closing and locking the door as the tenant left, and she watched as he returned to her side.

'Give me the contact number.'

She didn't pretend to misunderstand, and she retrieved a card from her pocket and gave it to him, watching as he made the call on his phone.

There were terse, hard words as Wolfe made arrangements to pay her debt in full at a mutually agreed time and place.

He slid the phone into his jacket pocket, and retrieved his wallet. 'What do you owe on this place?'

The rent was paid in advance and up to date. It had to be, or personal belongings were held for a week, then both tenant and belongings were out on the street.

She attempted to speak, heard the croaking sound, and resorted to hand signals, watching as he anchored a large bill beneath her room-key on the scarred dresser.

The room was spartan, comprising a single bed, a dresser and chair, and a tiny wardrobe. There were shared bathrooms, a shared kitchen at the end of the hallway and a communal lounge. A laundry was situated in a separate building out back of the house.

'You have a bag?'

Lara spared him a startled look.

'For your belongings,' Wolfe elaborated. 'You're not staying here.'

She was tired, jumpy with nerves, and she shook her head in a defenceless gesture. Where could she go at this time of night?

'My hotel,' he informed her as if she'd spoken, and her eyes blazed as she opened her mouth, then closed it again, aware that anything she said would emerge as an indistinguishable refusal.

He opened the small free-standing wardrobe, removed a capacious sports bag and placed it on the single bed.

Lara rose to her feet as he began opening drawers, refusing to have him go through her things.

Not that it had the slightest effect, as she battled with him in transferring contents from the wardrobe and dresser-drawers.

It didn't take long, and when they were done he took hold of the bag, indicated the door, and followed her out to the Lexus.

Any words seemed superfluous, and they rode the arterial route into the inner city in silence, reaching the Darling Harbour hotel, where the concierge organized valet-parking while Wolfe collected her bag.

Lara accompanied him as he bypassed Reception and headed towards a bank of lifts, and when the doors of one slid open he indicated she precede him, then he hit the button for a high floor.

She prayed that he didn't intend her to share his suite. Or, if he did, she hoped it contained two beds, or at least a sofa.

'Relax.' His voice held a drawling quality minutes later as he swiped a keycard into the slot.

Sure, and she could do that?

'I'd prefer a room of my own.' The words were hopelessly husky, even to her own ears.

'Accept it's not going to happen. Your security is paramount until the loan shark is paid off.'

'But—'

'It isn't subject to negotiation,' Wolfe said hardly.

'I don't want to share with you,' she attempted to convey.

His gaze lanced her own, his eyes darkly obdurate. 'Deal with it, Lara. At the moment seduction isn't on the agenda.'

That was supposed to be reassurance?

It was a large suite, Lara registered as he flicked on the lights, with two queen-size beds…a minor concession in the scheme of things.

A fleeting glance revealed there were two comfortable chairs positioned close to a wall of glass, shaded by floor-to-ceiling drapes. A small table and two serviceable dining chairs, a desk containing a fax machine, internet connection, the requisite television console, mini-bar.

Wolfe deposited her bag, then he crossed to the bedside phone, dialled Reception and requested medical assistance.

Lara shook her head and croaked a definitive, 'No,' only to be subjected to a raking appraisal.

'A doctor on call, or the accident-and-emergency ward of a private hospital. Choose.'

The thought of attending the latter—the form-filling, the inevitable questions—held little appeal, and she shrugged, too wound up to argue with him.

'Sit down.'

She watched as he removed his jacket, collected a hand towel, extracted ice from the mini-fridge, assembled a cold-pack and placed it along her jaw line.

'Keep it there.'

Wolfe crossed to the buffet and set the electric kettle to heat.

She was briefly aware of his impressive breadth of shoulder, the economical ease of movement as he completed the task.

A few minutes later he handed her a cup and saucer, then he took a nearby chair and regarded her steadily.

She sipped and cautiously swallowed the hot, sweet tea, and waited several seconds before repeating the action.

'Is there anything else you haven't told me?' Wolfe queried silkily.

'No.' Lara closed her eyes, then slowly opened them again, all too aware how foolish she'd been in not calling the loan shark before leaving the restaurant.

'It wouldn't have made any difference. You were out of time, and loan sharks are notorious for their hardline tactics.'

Her eyes widened as they met his.

He read minds?

Or was hers transparent?

'Drink your tea. A doctor should be here soon.'

'Soon' seemed an age, although it couldn't have been more than ten minutes before an imperious knock on the door heralded the doctor's arrival.

Credentials were offered, introductions completed. The answering of a few pertinent questions and an examination resulted in the assurance her larynx wasn't damaged, the bruising would duly emerge and subside, and her voice should return to normal by morning.

He handed over a sample pack of painkillers and a sedative, accepted his fee and left.

Lara unpacked a few essentials and headed into the *en*

suite. A shower helped ease some of the tension, and she enjoyed the luxury of a seemingly endless supply of hot water…so different from the boarding house, where an inadequate hot-water system meant lukewarm ablutions.

Dry, she pulled on a large cotton tee-shirt, added briefs, caught her hair together in a single plait, completed her nightly routine, then emerged to find Wolfe waiting for her, pills and a glass of water in hand.

'Take these, then go to bed. You're beat.'

Oh great. As if she needed to be reminded of her mirrored image, the dark, dilated eyes in a waxen, pale face.

Without a word she took the pills and swallowed each one cautiously with water, then she slid beneath the covers on the bed closest to the external glass-wall.

'Thanks.' A huskily voiced word meant to encompass much.

Wolfe inclined his head as he switched off the lights with the exception of a lamp on the desk, then he opened his laptop and soon became engrossed with data on-screen.

Lara closed her eyes and willed the medication to take effect as she relived walking into the house, making the phone call in the hallway…her assailant appearing out of nowhere and the resultant fracas.

It was all too easy to feel a hand gripping the top of her throat, the resultant pain and pressure as he lifted and slammed her hard against the wall…and the fear.

A shiver shook her slim frame, and she unconsciously curled her body into a protective ball.

She was here with Wolfe, and safe.

But for how long?

Soon she'd become his wife, and face another hurdle…that of sharing his life without allowing herself the benefit of emotional attachment.

Difficult, when she had vivid recall of the frankly sensual touch of his mouth on her own, and the electrifying passion he'd effortlessly aroused. It had blown her away, and had become an unconscious benchmark which sadly no other man had matched.

So where did that leave her?

It suddenly became too difficult to think, and her breathing slowed as she was claimed by sedative-induced sleep… unaware of the man who worked a little longer, showered, then slid in between the covers of the other bed.

CHAPTER FOUR

LARA became aware of light, when her subconscious expected darkness, and there was the tantalizing drift of fresh coffee teasing the air as she shifted in bed and slowly opened her eyes.

The hotel suite, Wolfe… Each descended in a heartbeat.

The small banker's-lamp glowed on the desk where Wolfe was seated, keying data into his laptop.

What was the time? Her watch…where was it?

She checked the bedside pedestal, saw the offending time-piece and snatched it up.

Six.

The markets. She was in danger of missing the early-morning fish market.

In one swift movement she threw back the bedcovers and rose to her feet, then she quickly pulled on jeans and dragged on a sweatshirt.

'What do you think you're doing?'

Wolfe's silky drawl drew a fraught glance in his direction as she slid her feet into trainers.

'Going to the fish market,' she said without thought to her voice, or its return. 'I should have been there an hour ago.'

The sedative she'd taken had to have been responsible for her sleeping through the alarm. Or, she reflected hurriedly, given the night's events, had she even remembered to activate it?

Whatever; it hardly mattered. Her main priority was to reach the markets before the fishermen loaded up their catch and began their deliveries.

'Call in an order.'

'That's not how I choose my supplies.'

Deft fingers smoothed her hair into a ponytail, then she reached for her jacket, collected her shoulderbag and crossed the room. Only to find Wolfe blocking her way.

Clad in jeans and a cotton tee-shirt, he exuded a raw masculinity…heightened by the fact he had yet to shave, and the dark stubble added a primitive air she endeavoured to ignore.

'Enlighten me.'

'Personal selection ensures good quality,' she elaborated. 'And I prefer wholesale to retail prices.'

He let his gaze travel over her features. 'You've had less than five hours' sleep.'

'So what else is new?' She wanted to hit him, and for a brief second she considered it. Except there was a warning stillness that boded ill for any retaliatory action.

'Can we have this argument later, rather than *now*?'

Without a further word he shrugged into a jacket, collected keys, wallet, and the room keycard. 'Let's go.'

She opened her mouth to protest, then closed it again and followed him out to the bank of lifts.

Lara was aware of the concierge calling up Wolfe's car, whereupon she gave Wolfe directions as they traversed slick wet streets, and a short while later they caught sight of fishmongers loading what was left of the catch.

Without a word she slid from the car and hailed two men by name as she raced towards them.

Wolfe cut the engine and emerged into the cool morning air, to lean lazily against the Lexus as Lara went into action, watching as she offered apologies and issued a plea to view and select her restaurant's daily order of fresh fish, lobster, local crustaceans and prawns.

Wolfe witnessed the men's expressions change from irritation to philosophical acceptance, and glimpsed Lara's answering smile as they conceded her choices.

A short while later Lara returned to the car, and he straightened to his full height.

'I gather you saved the day.'

She had, at wholesale prices. The alternative, if she'd been any later, would have meant buying at inflated retail cost. 'Thanks.'

'That's it?'

'For now.'

'Why do I get the feeling there's more?'

She crossed round to the passenger side, and relayed the day's schedule as she opened the door. 'I get to have an hour's sleep, grab breakfast and hit the restaurant around nine.'

He leaned an arm against the roof and regarded her carefully. 'Not today.'

'Today.' She slid into the seat, aware he copied her actions.

He fired the engine, and cast her a piercing look. 'It's not negotiable.'

'The hell it isn't.' Her eyes sparked blue fire as anger rose to the surface. 'Our *deal*, for want of a better word, begins when we sign the marriage certificate.' Which, God willing, wouldn't happen for another week or more at least.

She needed time to adjust to the idea of sleeping with him. Oh, *get it right*…intimacy. Even the mere thought elevated her pulse-rate and did strange things to her equilibrium.

If only she could indulge in the physical, and hold her emotions in check. Engage the body, but close out the mind.

Fat chance. He'd engaged her emotionally from the moment she'd first met him…something which hadn't changed in a decade.

And now she would soon take his name, share her body with his, and attempt to pretend it was OK.

The early-morning rain shower had ceased, and the grey dawn subsided as the sun began colouring the landscape.

Light traffic traversed the streets, and within minutes they reached the hotel.

'I'll go work out in the gym,' Wolfe indicated as he unlocked the suite.

Lara inclined her head as she toed off her trainers and shed her jacket, then she set her watch alarm and backed it up by requesting a wake-up call.

While she did that, he exchanged his jeans for sweats, caught up a towel and slung it over one shoulder, then he exited the suite as she crawled beneath the bedcovers.

A short morning nap was so much a part of her daily routine she was asleep within minutes.

The next thing she knew was the sound of the alarm buzzing in tandem with the insistent peal of the phone relaying her wake-up call, and she reached for the handset, closed the alarm, swung her legs out from the bed…and saw Wolfe unloading their breakfast tray onto the table.

'Hi.'

'You had no trouble sleeping?'

He'd showered, shaved and exchanged sweats for tailored trousers and a business shirt left unbuttoned at the neck.

'The habit of years,' Lara managed evenly.

He examined her features and the tumbled ash-blonde hair drifting onto each cheek. There was evidence of faint bruising beginning to emerge on the underside of her jawline, and he masked a momentary surge of anger.

With *her*, for neglecting to fill him in with the finer details of precisely who she'd owed money to and when it had been due for payment.

Wolfe pointed at the table. 'Come and eat while the food is hot.'

Lara rose to her feet in one fluid movement and automatically loosened the tie holding her hair in place. 'Give me a few minutes.'

She collected fresh clothes and attempted to ignore the way her stomach executed a backwards flip as she moved past him.

He disturbed her more than she was prepared to admit, and there was a sense of temporary relief as she reached the *en suite*.

In a matter of minutes she was done, and she emerged feeling better equipped to face whatever the day might bring.

Lara couldn't pinpoint the last time she'd had a cooked breakfast, and she slid into a chair as Wolfe joined her at the table.

Coffee—hot, black and sweet—was liquid ambrosia, and she forked a portion of eggs Benedict, savoured it, then continued eating with renewed appetite.

'First up this morning is a legal appointment,' Wolfe began. 'Followed by various real-estate inspections.'

'You intend buying a house?'

'We need somewhere to live.'

The plural 'we' caused sensation to spiral deep inside, and she took a soothing sip of coffee, then carefully placed the cup down onto its saucer. There was the home Darius and Suzanne had shared…

'No,' Wolfe refuted quietly, accurately reading her thought pattern. 'That isn't a consideration.'

If he insisted on adding to his property portfolio, why should she attempt to argue?

'After lunch we'll fit in some shopping before I meet with Darius' managerial staff.'

He worked fast, she accorded silently. Although what else did she expect?

Her chin lifted a little as she met his gaze and held it. 'You could have checked with me first. The restaurant is operating on minimum staff. I *have* to be there. There's no one else to take my place at such short notice.'

Wolfe's gaze narrowed. 'Find someone.'

'Sure.' Her eyes blazed a brilliant blue. 'I'll just wave a magic wand and, *poof*, a sous chef will appear out of nowhere, ready to start—' she checked her watch '—in half an hour.'

His expression didn't change, and the smooth silkiness in his voice held a silent warning. 'Take care of it, Lara.'

'Or *you* will?'

One eyebrow lifted in silent cynicism. 'Yes.'

Time out for a deep breath or three. 'Hiring someone,' she managed with attempted calm, 'is my responsibility.'

'Make it a priority. A celebrant will conduct our marriage on Sunday morning, after which we fly to New York.'

Her stomach executed a quick somersault and refused to settle. 'Excuse me?'

Wolfe leaned back in his chair and regarded her steadily. 'You heard.'

The nerves deep inside pulled tight almost to the point of pain, and she pushed her plate aside. 'Do I have a choice?'

'No.'

Succinct, adamant and spoken with an indolence that made her wary.

'Why? My presence in New York will be totally unnecessary. You'll be wheeling and dealing by day, and—'

'Sharing your bed at night.'

Did hearts stop? She was willing to swear hers had. What was more, for several long seconds it seemed her whole body shut down. Then she remembered to breathe.

'Payback time,' she managed. 'How could I have forgotten?'

'Should I be flattered or flattened?'

Lara summoned a deliberate smile. 'Flattened, definitely.'

His faint laughter sent goosebumps scudding down her spine. A reaction she refused to examine in any detail.

In order to survive, living with Wolfe would mean adopting a façade. Something she shouldn't find too difficult, given she'd had practice presenting a sociable mask on the occasion she'd found herself in Wolfe's presence.

'Finish your coffee.' He checked his watch. 'We need to leave.' Without a further word he crossed to the console and collected a set of keys.

She wanted to protest, and almost did. Except one look into those dark grey eyes was sufficient warning she couldn't win.

He moved in close and pressed a forefinger to her lips. 'Don't push it.'

Within minutes she slid her feet into comfortable shoes, applied lipgloss, then caught up her shoulderbag and accompanied Wolfe from the suite.

The legalities were straightforward; the lawyer's explanation merely endorsed Wolfe's instructions, and the pre-nuptial agreement drawn at Lara's insistence absolved Wolfe from providing her with anything other than a home, and a generous allowance. Any children issuing from the marriage would become their joint financial responsibility.

Signatures were applied to various documentation and duly witnessed, the lawyer offered his congratulations and best wishes…and it was done.

Sunday. Dear heaven. *Five days.*

Don't think about it, she cautioned silently as she accompanied Wolfe down to the car. Just take what each day throws at you, and achieve what you can.

Not the best scenario for someone who coveted perfection in most things. Especially finding a suitable sous chef in so short a time.

Or the number of things quickly escalating in her mind as Wolfe eased the Lexus out of its parking bay.

'Is there a close relative you'd like to witness our civil ceremony on Sunday? Your father, perhaps?'

Suzanne had been an only child; there were no aunts, uncles or cousins. Just her father…a man who'd declined to attend his ex-wife's funeral, and was unlikely to accept an invitation to his daughter's wedding.

'No.'

It didn't take long to reach the Rocks, and she released the safety belt as soon as he slid to a halt adjacent to her restaurant.

She reached for the door latch. 'Thanks.'

'Call my mobile phone when you're done for the evening.'

Lara paused in the process of closing the passenger door, a refusal on the tip of her lips, only to have him lean towards her.

'Do it, Lara,' he reiterated, and she simply pushed the door closed and filched a set of keys from her bag.

The rest of the day proved hectic, with a discrepancy in produce supplies necessitating phone calls and an adjustment to the lunch menu.

The title 'chef', in Lara's instance, covered a broad spectrum as she checked food preparation, utilized her cooking skills, took care of business, and ensured everything ran smoothly to plan.

Temperament, swearing and hissy fits were not tolerated, and the motto in her kitchen varied from 'just do it', 'suck it up', to 'customer satisfaction rules'.

The team comprised junior chefs and wait staff who worked well together, surmounting the inevitable daily hiccup with minimum angst and occasional humour.

By early afternoon Lara had apprised the staff of her temporary absence in New York, her marriage, and provided assurance their jobs were secure.

News which both Shontelle and Sally refused to accept

without voiced concern, and they urged a confrontation as the staff returned to their positions.

'Like, why…and why the rush?' Sally quietly demanded.

'Wolfe has to get back to New York, and he wants to get married before we leave.'

'I can go with that. Except there are holes in the overall story,' Shontelle pursued with a faint frown.

'Uh-huh,' Sally agreed. 'You're not exactly the ecstatic, starry-eyed bride-to-be. So what gives?'

They deserved her honesty, for they'd worked together, shared much, and had provided unstinting support when Paul, her business partner, had left her financially bereft.

Lara provided the expurgated version, encapsulating it in one sentence, and went on to explain, 'I hated that my trust in Paul was totally misplaced…ashamed he managed to fool me so successfully. I've fought hard to hold on to Lara's… something I couldn't have managed without your support, and your willingness to go that extra mile for me,' she added with sincerity. 'I care for Wolfe, and I know he's an honourable man with whom I'll share a pleasant life. Our forthcoming marriage is a sensible solution,' she concluded.

'And you're OK to settle with *sensible*?' Sally queried with concern. 'If he gives you grief, he'll pay—big time,' Sally promised.

Shontelle added fiercely, 'When do we get to meet him?'

'For the visual once-over and a verbal third degree?' Lara teased.

A few phone calls resulted in two interviews arranged for mid-afternoon, each applicant presenting an impressive CV…although proof involved follow-up calls to their current or previous employers, which if satisfactory then relied heavily upon a hands-on trial. Something she organized to occur over the next two consecutive days.

Evening reservations ensured efficient handling in the kitchen. Not an easy task when operating on minimum staff.

However, they managed—just—and shortly after nine the orders for mains lessened and progressed towards desserts and coffee.

'Party of five, and a gorgeous hunk—solo,' Sally imparted with an appreciative rolling of her eyes as she presented their order. 'On a score of one to ten, he's an eleven.'

Lara merely lifted speculative eyebrows, checked the order and set to filling it.

Sally made a humorous game of according scores to the attractive men frequenting the restaurant.

'Going to spread some charm.' Sally grinned as she filched a bottle of still water from the display refrigerator then exited the kitchen.

Good luck, Lara offered silently as she seared a medallion of eye-fillet steak, selected the appropriate sauce and arranged the accompanying salad.

'Think I'm in love,' Sally enthused when she returned, and Lara shot her a telling look. 'Yeah, I know. Like he's going to even *look* at me. But a girl can fantasize.' A telling sigh emerged, accompanied by a feigned dreamy expression.

'You're a riot.'

Sally offered an infectious grin as she collected the order. 'Helps pass the time, darling.'

So it did. Lightening the load when stress threatened to reach the stratosphere, as it did, for one reason or another, on a reasonably regular basis.

Lara had worked the evening with efficient speed, clearing her mind of everything except the essential need to pay attention to detail, and the individual touches that made each dish on the menu special.

Events of the past few days were beginning to take their toll, and she rolled her shoulders in an attempt to ease the muscles in her upper body. Battling a tension headache didn't help, and she looked forward to closing down for the night and sinking into bed.

Last night a medically prescribed sedative had ensured a good night's sleep. What would the coming night bring?

Oh, for heaven's sake! Take a reality check!

Sex with Wolfe was a given. It was just a matter of *when*. *So get over it!*

He was a man…like any other.

Sure he is.

A mental, mischievous little imp laughed uproariously until she silently chastised and banished him.

Lara stifled a faintly audible groan, and her hands flew as she gathered a dessert plate, cut a perfect portion of cheesecake, drizzled tangy strawberry sauce in a decorative pattern, added fresh flute-cut strawberries and placed the plate on the serving shelf.

Soon Sally would be able to handle the orders for tea and coffee, and Gina could move into the kitchen to help clean up.

Lara glanced towards the door as Shontelle entered the kitchen and moved close. 'Compliments to the chef from gentleman at table seven.'

OK, so she'd swing by, smile, exchange a few words with their regular clientele and acknowledge the compliment.

It took a few minutes as she paused at one table, then another—until she saw just *who* was seated at table seven.

Wolfe, *here*? What game was he playing?

'Don't tell me,' she managed equably as she reached his side. 'You were at a loose end, and decided to observe my restaurant first-hand?'

'No. I finished late, hadn't eaten and decided to dine here instead of ordering room service.'

She tilted her head to one side. 'I guess that'll fly.'

'Join me for coffee.'

She offered a slight mock-curtsy. 'The kitchen awaits.'

A faint smile teased the edge of his mouth. 'I'll take a rain check.'

He did, until the last patron left, then Lara had no option but to effect an introduction to the remaining staff—which, she suspected, had been his intention—and at his request Shontelle retrieved two bottles of champagne.

The celebratory toast was almost surreal. So too were the voiced congratulations.

'*Wow*,' Sally accorded in a quiet aside. 'His score exceeds ten, twice over. I hereby withdraw almost all reservations.'

It was midnight when Lara closed and locked the restaurant. Wolfe's black Lexus was stationary at the kerb, and Lara evinced concern as Sally bade them goodnight.

'Are you sure you'll be OK?'

'I've been taking the late train since for ever,' Sally assured. 'Long before you moved into the same street.'

Wolfe indicated the Lexus. 'We'll give you a ride.'

The city never slept, it merely quieted down some, traffic lessened. The distance to Darlinghurst was achieved in minimum time, during which Sally, bless her, never let the conversation lull.

'Thanks. See you tomorrow.'

Wolfe waited to engage the transmission until Sally disappeared indoors, and Lara leaned back against the head-rest as he turned the car towards the inner city.

She was conscious of Wolfe's appraisal later as the hotel lift sped quickly to their high floor.

'You didn't need to wait until the restaurant closed. I could have caught a train.'

'Do you particularly want to argue?' Wolfe queried as he slid the keycard into place and opened the door.

Right at that minute all she wanted to do was shed her clothes, take a long, hot shower, then tumble into bed.

'No.'

'Wise.' Wolfe tossed keys onto the bedside pedestal, then shrugged out of his jacket.

Lara toed off her shoes, then she collected her nightwear and moved into the *en suite*.

It was bliss to stand beneath the spray of steaming water and let it ease out the kinks, and it was several long minutes before she picked up the soap, lathered and rinsed it off.

Wolfe was standing at the desk, scrolling through data on his laptop, when she emerged into the room, and he pressed 'save' then closed down.

He noted her pale features, the dark circles beneath her eyes. 'Take something for that headache.'

'I don't need you to play nurse.' *Or my keeper*, she added silently. Except that was precisely what he'd become. Rescuing her from certain personal and financial disaster.

His eyes darkened a little, and her pulse kicked into a faster beat as he moved close.

'I trust you've organized your replacement?'

Lara closed her eyes against the sight of him, then slowly opened them again. 'You want to exchange a recap of each other's day?'

'A simple yes or no will do.'

His silky-voiced drawl shivered the length of her spine, and her chin tilted a little in silent defiance. 'Two interviews, with two trials over the next two consecutive nights. Satisfied?'

'Not entirely.'

Fleeting indecision shadowed her eyes, then it was gone. 'Tough.'

He covered the few steps necessary to reach her, and she viewed him warily as he lifted a hand to tuck a wayward lock of hair behind her ear, then she swallowed compulsively as he trailed gentle fingers down one cheek.

'What are you doing?'

The edges of his mouth curved a little as he lowered his mouth to hover a mere inch from her own. 'You need to ask?'

His lips brushed hers, teased a little, and her heartbeat leapt as he traced the lower curve with the tip of his tongue, then ventured in to begin an erotic tasting that attacked her resistance and tore it to shreds.

She felt his hands slip beneath her tee-shirt and cup the slight curve of her buttocks, squeeze a little, then one hand slid up over her ribcage to capture her breast.

A faint groan emerged from her throat as he brushed one tender peak, then rolled it gently between thumb and forefinger.

Wolfe felt his senses quicken, and he deepened the kiss as he sought her response, caught the hitch in her breath and her capitulation. And he wanted more...so much more.

His arousal was a potent force, and he sought the soft curls at the apex of her thighs, the moist heat there...and felt her body go rigid.

He stilled as she wrenched his mouth from his own, and when she pushed against him he released her to arm's length.

'Please—don't.'

His eyes narrowed and became impossibly dark. 'That wasn't the message you were giving me mere seconds ago.'

Because she'd craved his touch and didn't think! Damn it, she'd never been able to think when he was anywhere close.

Something he'd always known, and she was willing to swear he'd taken pleasure in taunting her vulnerable emotions with a look, the touch of his hand, the light teasing brush of his lips to her cheek in welcome whenever he'd flown in from the States. The occasional kiss that came close to getting out of hand...

The times she'd taken his actions as deliberate...and hated him afresh for it.

'A few days, Wolfe,' Lara reminded him. 'Will it be such a hardship to wait until I have your ring on my finger?'

He inclined his head. 'If you insist.'

It hurt that he acquiesced so easily.

Sex, she reflected a trifle bitterly. *That's all it is to him. So get over it.*

Without a further word she crossed to the large bed she'd nominated as her own, lifted the covers and slid beneath them.

Habit ensured she activated the alarm on her watch, and her eyes widened as he began shedding his clothes.

For a moment she was transfixed by the sight of him, the smooth flex of rippling muscle and sinew with each movement, as he pulled his shirt free from his trousers and discarded it.

Next he loosened his belt, undid the clasp at his waist and slid down the zip fastening.

Oh hell, she was no voyeur, and her lashes swept down, remaining closed until she heard the faint rustle of bedclothes as he occupied his bed.

'You're quite safe.'

His faintly inflected drawl held a tinge of amusement, and she turned to look at him as he crossed his arms above his head.

She was aware of the faint drift of exclusive cologne, the faint, male muskiness… The pulse at the base of her throat leapt to a faster beat.

Safe?

Did he have any idea how her body reacted to him? All her skin cells seemed alive and begging his touch. Something she found difficult to control, and totally at variance with the dictates of her brain.

'The loan shark has been paid off.'

'Thank you.'

She should feel relieved, and she did.

Really.

Except, with every step she took, it felt as if she was merely exchanging one form of debt for another.

CHAPTER FIVE

THE alarm and wake-up call sounded simultaneously, and Lara deactivated her watch as Wolfe reached for the phone.

His upper body was bare to the waist. Gleaming tanned skin pulled taut over superb musculature that rippled fluidly with every move. She caught a brief glimpse of exposed buttock, and momentarily froze.

Her gaze met his, and for an unguarded moment she resembled a startled doe.

Wolfe's eyes darkened and became thoughtful as he replaced the receiver and swung back to his side of the bed.

It was a long time since he'd shared a room with a woman where sex hadn't featured throughout the night. A sophisticated, willing partner who knew the score…and, when the relationship concluded, accepted the appropriate gift with no hard feelings.

Yet *this* was different, without precedent.

Until now, marriage hadn't formed part of his agenda.

Risk taking, following his instincts and acting on them, was part of who he was. In the cut and thrust of tough business deals, he'd surprised his competitors…and at times, himself…by winning against incredible odds. It had also made him a very wealthy man, with enviable share-and-property portfolios, and was something of a legend for his business nous.

On Monday he'd entered Darius' lawyer's sanctum with no intention other than learning the contents of his late father's will. Yet within the space of a few hours he'd made a series of life-changing decisions.

Based on what?

A young woman's air of fragility that meshed with strength, pride and resolve. The memory of a teenaged girl whose lips had melted against his own…warm, giving and innocent. His sudden and totally unexpected reaction.

Impossible.

It was a decision based on loyalty to his father. An attempt to make amends for following his own path, instead of agreeing to the one Darius had set for him.

The marriage clause was contestable and unlikely to stand up in a court of law…yet he'd chosen to concede to the written dictum.

With Lara…the daughter of Darius' second wife, a young woman far removed from his usual intimate companions. Someone who'd won Darius' affection and had returned it in kind, refusing, as had Suzanne, financial help in achieving her goals. Evidenced by legal proof…a fact which had surprised him and soon destroyed his previous misconceptions.

Even now, with every passing day, Lara continually battled for independence.

Unless she was a skilled actress, which he seriously doubted, she hated relying on him for anything.

Lara gathered up fresh underwear, jeans, tee-shirt and disappeared into the *en suite*, to emerge soon after to discover Wolfe dressed and in the process of pouring coffee into two cups.

'There's no need—' *for you to come with me…* Except one hard look in her direction ensured she didn't finish the sentence.

'We did this yesterday,' Wolfe drawled. 'Let's not do it again.' He held out a cup and saucer. 'Coffee. Black, two sugars. Drink it, then we'll hit the road.'

There was the temptation to tell him what to do with the coffee, and only the need for a caffeine fix prevented a verbal comeback.

The fact he knew irked her, and she opted for silence during the short drive to the fish market, where she made her selections, haggled a little, smiled when she beat down the price and executed a high-five gesture with a competitor.

'Negotiations are in place on a property at Point Piper,' Wolfe informed her as they shared breakfast.

One of Sydney's luxury harbour-front suburbs, she acknowledged. Expensive—make that *very* expensive—real estate.

'I've arranged for a firm of interior decorators to quote on refurbishment. Ideally, it'll completed by the time we return from New York.'

Why should she be surprised? Money, enough of it, could achieve almost anything.

'I'll collect you at two-thirty this afternoon.'

Lara opened her mouth to argue, only to close it again as Wolfe continued, 'And have you back at the restaurant by four. Your staff assured me they'll manage.'

'You arranged this without first checking with me?'

'I merely circumvented your objection.'

So he had, with sufficient finesse that left her no quarter but to concede…or sound like a petulant child.

'Do all women of your acquaintance fall at your feet, eager to fulfil your every wish?'

The corners of his mouth curved with humour. 'What an interesting concept.'

'You didn't answer the question.'

He inclined his head. 'More often than *not*.'

Lara offered him a sweet smile. 'Count me among the not.'

'Indeed?'

He was amused, damn him!

'It'll be a refreshing change,' she assured him.

Wolfe's husky chuckle curled round her nerve-ends and tugged a little. 'I foresee we'll share an...*interesting* marriage.'

The mere thought sent her emotions into sensual over-drive, and she consciously tamped them down. If she allowed him to see the degree of her emotional vulnerability, she'd be lost.

And that would never do.

Lara refrained from offering any comment as she drained her coffee, then she stood to her feet and gathered up her shoulderbag.

'I have to leave.'

Wolfe reached the door as she did, and she opened her mouth to protest, only to incur his dark look.

'Give it up, Lara.'

'Two-thirty,' Wolfe reminded as he drew the Lexus to a halt outside the restaurant.

OK, so she'd go look at the house.

How difficult could it be?

It was the usual morning rush, with the need to check de-liveries, make any last-minute menu changes, ensure out-standing bills were paid, and elevate Shontelle to the position of manager.

Lunch orders involved coordination, deft speed and, with luck, no hiccups.

Mercifully, there was only one picky customer who insisted she'd ordered a caesar salad with anchovies, not smoked salmon. Freshly assembled, it was sent back again only to meet a complaint she'd requested dressing on the side.

Sally merely executed an expressive eye-roll. 'I'll ask for a precise count of cos leaves, the number of croutons, anchovy fillets, with bacon bits or without, parmesan on the side or sprinkled...or perhaps the customer would like *all* the ingre-dients brought to the table separately so she can assemble the salad to her satisfaction?' She offered a feline smile. 'Offered with the utmost politeness, of course.'

Lara sent her an exasperated look. 'Must you?'

'Watch me.'

Within minutes Sally was back, a grin widening her generous mouth. 'We have a winner.'

At two-twenty-five Lara removed her apron, tidied her hair and secured it with a large clip, applied lipgloss, collected her shoulderbag and moved through the swing-door separating the kitchen from the restaurant.

Wolfe stood at the front desk, engaged in conversation with Shontelle.

Attired in tailored black trousers and a white collarless shirt over which he wore a black butter-soft leather jacket, he stood with the ease of a man comfortable in his own skin, assured and able to deal with anything that came his way.

Steadily he was taking over her life, presenting options and choices which held validity, but in reality provided her with no choice at all.

Lara wove her way past tables and paused as she reached his side. Only to have the breath catch in her throat beneath the warmth of his smile as he lowered his head and brushed his lips to her cheek.

'Ready?'

Oh my. The show of affection had to have been for Shontelle's benefit...and anyone who happened to be watching.

She could do bright, friendly, even warm. However, anything resembling flirting was out.

'Let's go.'

He caught hold of her hand and threaded his fingers through her own. Something which elevated her nervous tension, and she waited until they reached the kerb before attempting to wrench her hand free.

'Isn't the hand-holding thing a bit over the top?'

Wolfe disarmed the locking mechanism and opened the passenger door. 'It bothers you?'

Yes. The word became locked in her throat as a silent scream. 'Of course not,' she managed evenly as she slid into the seat.

In the confines of the car she was supremely conscious of him, the aura of power and masculine strength he exuded mingling with the unobtrusive drift of expensive cologne.

His hands on the wheel were sure, his control of the Lexus total, as he handled the traffic with ease through the city streets, soon connecting with the New South Head Road leading towards Point Piper.

It was a lovely spring day with a tinge of warmth in the sun as it bathed the harbour and encroaching suburbs.

Mansions, some gracious others modern, stood behind high walls with steel-gated frontages.

Most were worth a veritable fortune, and owned by the rich and famous who coveted their privacy.

There was a sense of curiosity as Wolfe eased the car to a halt behind a late-model Mercedes, the owner of which moved forward to provide an expansive greeting as soon as Wolfe emerged from the Lexus.

'My fiancée, Lara Sommers,' Wolfe introduced smoothly as he crossed to the agent's side, and she felt the light pressure of Wolfe's hand at the back of her waist as they entered the house.

An action which suddenly made her conscious of a need to regulate her breathing.

Which was crazy.

The house…concentrate on the house, she bade silently as they passed through the large entrance with its marble-tiled floors, the beautiful neutral colours enhanced by individual features and exquisite lighting.

Built on three levels, the interior provided a guest suite, master suite, plus five bedrooms, each with an *en suite*, a formal and informal lounge and dining room, media room, office and library, together with utilities. There was garaging for three vehicles and a self-contained flat for live-in staff.

It was the kitchen which held her interest, for she'd worked in several over the years, and design layout and appliance placement were essential for maximum ease of use.

When it came to stove tops she preferred gas. For aesthetic purposes, the long, sweeping marble bench-tops provided a clean, simple look.

Outside, the grounds were landscaped to perfection, with beautifully clipped topiary, decorative flower beds and, situated at the rear, a gorgeous infinity-pool.

Panoramic views over the harbour were stunning by day, and undoubtedly a fairyland of light by night.

'What do you think?' Wolfe queried as they descended the curved stairway to the main entrance lobby.

'It's a beautiful home,' Lara acknowledged. 'Situated in a good location.'

'I should have a general overview from the interior decorators within a few days.'

No doubt the fee he was paying ensured the work would be accorded priority.

'What do you plan on having done?' she ventured as he eased the Lexus towards the New South Head Road.

'Upgrade the security system. Installation of a home gym. The interior re-painted throughout.' He spared her a quick glance. 'The kitchen is your territory. You'll have *carte blanche* to remodel it to your specifications.'

'It's a home, not a restaurant. There is a difference.'

'But you'd prefer to make some changes.'

'And you know this because…?'

'You have an expressive face.'

And here she was thinking she'd been particularly circumspect. 'The kitchen is perfectly adequate.'

'Adequate isn't enough.'

'You want perfection? It'll cost.'

'Work out a ballpark figure.'

'Just like that?'

'Yes. Just like that.'

His lazy drawl held amusement, and she drew in a deep breath. 'You could regret it.'

'Surprise me.'

Go for broke? She could do that, easily.

Wolfe deposited her outside the restaurant a few minutes before four.

'I'll take a cab to the hotel when I finish for the night,' Lara indicated as she reached for the door clasp.

'And deny me the opportunity to—'

'Play the part?'

'Of caring fiancé?' His eyes gleamed with musing humour. 'Indulge me.'

She threw him a cynical look. 'I'd prefer to think you enjoy the food.'

In one fluid movement she stepped from the car and closed the door with a refined click. Then she offered a mock salute and crossed the pavement.

Sassy, Wolfe accorded as he watched her walk away from him.

Petite, with a smart mouth, no artifice, and no longer an innocent.

Yet he made her nervous, apparent in the accelerated pulse-beat at the base of her throat. The soft tinge of pink that crept into her cheeks.

The knowledge intrigued him.

He moved the transmission into drive and checked the rear-vision mirror before moving out into the flow of traffic.

There were a number of calls he needed to make, a late-afternoon appointment, and he planned to fit in a workout in the hotel gym. Then he'd shower, dress and spend time on his laptop.

It was after nine when Wolfe eased the Lexus into a parking slot and entered Lara's. Shontelle greeted him warmly and showed him to a table.

'Wolfe just walked in.'

Lara cast Sally a harried glance, and immediately returned to the task at hand. 'Fine.' She glimpsed Sally's faintly lifted eyebrow and tempered it with, 'OK, thanks.'

It wasn't a good evening. The first of the two prospective chefs on trial wasn't working out too well. Twice the woman had stuffed up; although the errors were minor and could be attributed to nerves, it didn't make for an auspicious beginning.

Lara had painstakingly built up a reputation, and she refused to see it diminished in any way. Her existing staff were good workers, quick and incredibly loyal. Any newcomer had to meet with their approval as well as her own.

At ten, Lara bade the woman goodnight and promised to relay her decision within a few days.

The last patron left at eleven, the kitchen was restored to neatness, the tables cleared, and Sally retrieved the vacuum cleaner while Lara began locking up.

Wolfe lent a hand stacking chairs and they emerged into the cool night air to a light shower of rain, bade goodnight to Sally, who'd gained a lift from a fellow worker, then Wolfe eased the Lexus towards the inner city.

The almost silent swish of car tyres against wet bitumen was vaguely soothing, and she resisted the temptation to sink back against the head-rest and close her eyes.

'How did you rate tonight's trial with the first of the two replacement chefs?'

'It's better you don't ask.'

'That bad?'

She wanted to be fair, in spite of her reservations. 'I don't think she'll fit in with the team.'

Wolfe eased the Lexus into the hotel forecourt. 'Based on valid reason, or gut instinct?'

'Both.'

It was almost the witching hour when Wolfe inserted the keycard and unlocked their suite.

Lara toed off her trainers, gathered nightwear and moved into the *en suite*. A hot shower eased some of the evening's tension and, towelled dry, she pulled on a nightshirt, caught her hair together and emerged into the room.

Wolfe was in bed, his lengthy frame stretched out beneath the covers with both hands folded beneath his head. Dimly lit bedside lamps lent an intimacy she endeavoured to ignore... and failed miserably.

Just knowing he was *there*. Aware, if she moved a few paces, she could reach out and touch him. The nerves in her stomach curled into a tight ball at the thought of his possible reaction.

Oh, give it up, she silently derided as she slid into bed. Tonight...Sunday...next week. What was the difference?

She must have fallen asleep, for she woke to the sound of her watch alarm and the insistent peal of the phone heralding a wake-up call.

It became a day like any other, and Lara relaxed somewhat as the male chef on trial proved himself to be deft and skilled as he handled lunch with dedicated ease. The evening went equally well, and the kitchen team's approval cemented Lara's decision to hire him.

Anton—otherwise known as Anthony 'Tony' Smith from a small town out west—had trained in Sydney and worked in Europe. What was more, due to his recent return from a sojourn in France, he was available for an immediate start.

Like...tomorrow?

His, 'Why not? What time?' was easy.

There was nothing like having him dive in at the deep end. 'At the fish markets, before dawn.'

'I'll be there.'

He was, and together they bartered for the best supplies, secured and arranged for delivery, then settled on a time for him to report in to the restaurant.

'Free up a few hours this afternoon.' Wolfe inclined his head as they shared breakfast, and she spared him a wary look.

'Why?'

'Shopping.' He refilled his cup with coffee and leant back in his chair.

'I don't need anything.'

'Yes, you do,' he refuted easily. 'Unless you have a collection of clothes in storage?'

Her features paled beneath his steady gaze. 'I sold every designer label I owned in a bid to improve my cash flow.' Her chin lifted in silent defence. 'Not to mention paring down my belongings to a bare minimum.' She managed a cynical smile. 'Boarding houses aren't known for providing generous space for tenants' belongings.' Besides, given the long hours she worked, there was no time to socialize.

Pride, she possessed it in spades, together with a measure of integrity, he mused. 'Double Bay is close. We'll go there.'

'The hell we will.'

'Consider it an advance.'

'No,' Lara reiterated, hating the invidious position she was in.

'You dislike shopping?'

'I hate the thought of sinking even further into your debt.'

'Should I state the obvious?'

She tilted her head to one side. 'Where you relay the "most women" thing?' Her eyes sparked blue fire as she lifted a hand and began ticking off each finger. 'For the record, I'm not *most women*.' She took time to sweep his powerful frame from head to toe, and back again. 'Endorse your wealth? For your information, I don't give a fig.' Her expression tightened and a soft bloom of colour stained each cheekbone. 'Remind me I'll repay you with sex?'

One look into those dark eyes was enough to raise the hairs on the back of her neck, and she stood quickly to her feet…only to see him copy her action.

Oh, what was she doing?

Just as the thought 'play with fire and you get burnt' occurred, he reached for her and locked her body against his hard, muscular contours, making her startlingly aware of the strength and size of his arousal.

A startled gasp escaped from her lips as he held fast her head, then his mouth captured hers in a plundering possession that took hold of her emotions and shattered them.

A despairing groan rose and died in her throat as she curled her hand into a fist and aimed it for his shoulder.

Except his strength far outmatched her own, and he held her captive, gentling his invasion to something incredibly sensual, awakening her senses until he gained her unbidden response.

She lost all thought as he led her to a place where nothing else mattered…except the man, and his witching power to render her boneless.

For a wild moment she wanted more, so much more, and her hands unclenched as she linked them together at his nape, holding his head fast as she gave herself up to the magic of his touch.

Then it was he who began to withdraw, softening the contact as he nibbled her lower lip, savouring its faintly swollen contours, and lightly brushing her mouth with his own before gently breaking contact.

For a few timeless seconds she felt strangely adrift, then realization dawned and her eyes widened with stunned disbelief as she began fighting frantically to be free of him.

Except one powerful arm held her immobile while he took hold of her chin between finger and thumb, then he tipped it slightly so she had no recourse but to look at him…or close her eyes. And she refused to allow him the slightest sign of her defeat.

'In future you might care to consider my reaction before resorting to such a reckless turn of phrase,' Wolfe warned with indolent ease as he released her. 'Particularly if you want to enforce the "no sex before marriage" dictum.'

Not only *his* reaction but her own, Lara admitted wretchedly as she sought to put some distance between them.

Dear heaven…what had just happened here?

Déjà vu.

Except now it was worse, so much worse than she believed possible. She was older, wiser…and experienced. If you counted two brief liaisons and a vague disappointment in the sexual act, assigning the reason to her lack of emotional engagement for failing to achieve orgasm. Or had it been the result of selfish carelessness of the men in question?

Instinct warned it would be different when Wolfe took her to bed.

Just how different she'd discover within days…*nights*, she amended…aware there were only two remaining before she took his name and vowed to share his life.

Would he assume her compliance and seek to initiate sex tonight?

Even the thought that he might sent her into a wild emotional spin, and she barely controlled the myriad sensations sweeping through her body.

Right now she desperately needed to get away from him, and she took the few steps necessary to retrieve her shoulderbag.

'I'll take a cab.'

Wolfe merely ignored her and collected his keys as he followed her from the suite.

He waited until they were in the car and the Lexus purred

almost silently through the morning traffic before querying, 'Are you sufficiently confident in Tony's ability?'

'As much as I can be. Why?'

'Enough for you to finish up tonight?'

'Not possible. Saturday is our busiest day, not to mention the evening.'

'Need I remind you we marry Sunday morning, and board a flight to New York mid-afternoon?'

As if she could forget. 'Saturday stands.'

'And if I insist?'

'It won't make any difference,' Lara assured him, not willing to give so much as an inch.

The remaining short distance was achieved in silence, and Lara reached for the door-clasp the instant the car slid in against the kerb.

'Be ready at two o'clock,' Wolfe indicated in a voice as smooth as silk.

In your dreams, she managed silently. He could come drag her from the kitchen…if he dared.

In fact he did, if not quite literally, but with the enthused encouragement of Shontelle, Tony, and Sally… What choice did she have but to remove her apron and give in gracefully?

She even waited until they were safely in the car and out of earshot before railing at him for his high-handedness.

'Has no one accused you of being an arrogant, overbearing control-freak?'

'Aside from you? No.'

Her eyes darkened at the sound of amusement in his voice, and she pursed her lips in an effort to control the flood of words she felt compelled to throw at him.

Instead she concentrated on the scene beyond the windscreen, taking no pleasure in the sunshine, the almost cloudless blue skies, or the soft, budding flora unfolding with spring.

It didn't take long to reach the exclusive boutiques in

Double Bay, or for Wolfe to ease the Lexus into a convenient parking space.

'Let's go.'

Public mutiny wasn't part of her scene, and she slid from the car in silence then walked the pavement at his side.

The selection of wedding rings came first, and Lara tamped down a shocked gasp as he slid a wide multi-faceted diamond band onto her finger, then chose a gold band for himself.

The rings purchased and carefully boxed and bagged, Wolfe led her from one boutique to another until he approved a suitable dress in ivory with a delicate lace overlay...which happened to be her size. Matching stilettos were added at outrageous cost.

Not to be daunted, he included a set of ivory briefs and bra, showing no embarrassment whatsoever in choosing a preferred style.

'Have you no shame?' Lara demanded as they emerged onto the pavement. She barely refrained from stamping a foot in sheer frustration. '*Enough* already. I don't need anything else!'

'You do.' His lazy drawl curled round her nerve-ends and did strange things to her equilibrium. 'But it can wait.'

She should thank him, and she did, with such utmost graciousness it brought an amused smile in response.

'My pleasure.'

There was doubt what form such pleasure would take, and she fought against the quickening pulse beating at the base of her throat.

'Are we done?' She needed to immerse herself in the familiar and lose herself in work.

'Soon you won't be able to escape me so easily.'

Like she didn't know this?

'So I'll walk a little on the wild side,' Lara offered with deliberate facetiousness.

'You sound almost afraid.'

They reached the Lexus, and she sent him a sweet smile over the roof of the car. 'Shaking. Can't you tell?'

His husky chuckle sent the blood fizzing through her veins, and she deliberately ignored the exigent sexual energy as Wolfe delivered her to the restaurant.

'I'll take a cab to the hotel when I'm done,' Lara relayed as she released her safety-belt. 'With Tony on board, I may finish up earlier than usual.' She slid quickly from the car and walked towards the restaurant without a backwards glance.

CHAPTER SIX

TONY worked with skill, co-ordinating with everyone so well there was barely a hitch as the evening progressed. Lara felt some of the tension ease in the knowledge the restaurant would continue to operate quite well without her... although the thought of walking away from what represented years of hard work to reach eventual ownership would be a terrible wrench.

Lara's was her pride and joy, especially so in recent months, when she'd been forced to struggle against crippling odds to hold on to it, and then only by the skin of her teeth.

'Hey, get with the real world.'

Sally's light teasing broke the reflection, and Lara offered a self-deprecating smile.

'Wolfe's a gorgeous hunk any woman would kill to share body fluids with,' Sally declared with a mock-salacious grin. 'But right now I need a chocolate mousse, a bombe alaska, and a crème brûlée.'

A sudden flame flared deep inside at the image Sally's words evoked, and she resolutely dampened it down. 'Coming right up.'

'Why don't you call it a night?' Tony suggested a short while later. 'Sally and I'll close and lock up.'

An automatic refusal hovered on her lips, only to have him remind her, 'As from tomorrow, it'll be my responsibility.'

As difficult as it was to let go, she recognized it as something she had to do. 'You're sure?'

'Go. I'll take care of your baby as if it's my own.' He crossed his heart in a humorous gesture and offered a smile in reassurance. 'Promise.' A faintly wicked gleam lit his eyes. 'Take a rain check and sleep in. If you front up here tomorrow before late afternoon, you'll be in serious trouble.'

'My sentiments exactly.'

The drawl was familiar—too familiar—and Lara turned to see Shontelle had ushered Wolfe into the kitchen.

Tony glanced in Wolfe's direction. 'Your timing is perfect. I've just given Lara the rest of the night off.'

Wolfe's eyebrow slanted. 'And she accepted?'

'What is it with men, that they tend to stick together?' Lara posed to no one in particular.

'They need to, because women usually win,' Sally declared with a cheeky grin as she set up two glass plungers with coffee.

'Indeed?'

An icy chill slithered the length of Lara's spine at the faint mockery evident. No one could best a man of Wolfe's calibre…unless he chose to let them.

Controlled manipulation, honed by years of wheeling, dealing and building his own empire.

However, if he imagined he could employ similar tactics with *her*, he'd better forget it!

Almost as if he could discern her thoughts, he closed the distance between them and brushed his lips to her temple.

'Are you done?'

She managed a singularly sweet smile that didn't fool him in the slightest. 'For the evening, yes.'

'Then say goodnight and we'll leave.'

'Be still, my beating heart,' Sally offered with a grin, and Lara removed her apron, smoothed a hand over her hair, collected her shoulderbag, bade the staff goodnight and preceded Wolfe out onto the pavement.

'You were to call me when you finished for the evening,' Wolfe reminded her silkily as he put the Lexus in motion.

Lara spared him a careful look beneath the reflected street lighting. His broad-boned facial structure was arresting, and sculpted to chiselled perfection.

In such close proximity she couldn't help but be aware of him…the faint tones of his exclusive cologne, the expensive leather jacket. Not to mention the powerful male body beneath the freshly laundered clothing.

'Why, when I said I'd catch a cab?' she queried reasonably, and stifled the faint chill feathering the surface of her skin at the threat he posed to her emotional heart.

Verbal retaliation seemed her only defence, and there was a part of her that recognized the danger of going too far.

Hadn't he shown her the folly of doing so this morning?

The memory of how her mouth had felt following his invasion was too fresh for her to easily forget.

She owed him much. Too much.

Why rail against it…against him?

Yet she'd fought too hard for too long to slip into polite acquiescence.

Wolfe covered the distance between the Rocks and their hotel in silence, and as soon as they entered their suite Lara collected nightwear and headed for the shower.

When she emerged Wolfe had discarded his jacket and was seated at the small desk, intent on viewing data on his laptop.

Lara slid into bed…to sleep, hopefully within minutes, and not wake until morning.

She closed her eyes against the images swirling through her mind. For there had been so many changes in such a short time.

Too many, she reflected, aware of an aching sadness at the loss of her dearly loved mother, Suzanne, who'd been friend, confidante and there, kind and supportive as they'd shared the bad times. Never quite taking the good years for granted when Darius had taken them both beneath his wing.

Lara felt the faint burn of unshed tears in the knowledge Suzanne wouldn't witness her only daughter's wedding.

A painful lump rose in her throat and constricted there.

If Suzanne and Darius were alive, there wouldn't *be* a wedding.

She must have slept, for she was caught up in a terrible dream where she was travelling through France in an unfamiliar car, talking and laughing with Suzanne as they admired the passing scenery, and contemplating where they'd stop for the night. Darius favoured a hotel, while Suzanne inclined towards a family-owned bed and breakfast. Out of the blue a car careened at speed towards them, and Darius swung the wheel…then Lara became a disembodied spectator as the crash occurred, followed by an explosion…and she screamed. Crying out against the inevitability that no one could possibly survive the fiercely burning wreck…and again, begging a miracle against the cruel hand of fate as she ran towards the fiasco, felt the heat sear her body, and pushed at the hands that sought to pull her away.

'Lara.'

She barely registered someone calling her name, or the indistinct oath as she was hauled against a hard, warm body.

'Let me go!' She fought in earnest, desperate to be free.

The voice she dimly registered…it was familiar. And the hauntingly real scene gripping her mind began to fade, lingering on the fringes as it was superimposed by a lit room, recognition of the hotel suite, and the man who held her.

Wolfe.

His warm hard-muscled body…dear heaven, *naked*, she starkly registered as he trailed a soothing hand down her spine.

Tears welled up in her eyes and hovered there, threatening

to spill, then they overflowed to run in a slow rivulet down each cheek.

A husky oath escaped from his lips, and he lifted a hand to her cheek, gently brushing a thumb pad over one cheek, then the other.

'Easy, now.' His voice was quiet, almost soothing as he regarded her carefully, and there was a degree of concern apparent.

His breath teased the hair at her temple, tendrils that had escaped in her fierce struggle to be free of her nightmare captor, and her eyes dilated as he feathered the stray hair behind her ear.

Lara didn't think she was capable of uttering so much as a word.

The scene was surreal. Time stood still, encapsulated in a moment which seemed to stretch long as she processed the waiting, watchful quality apparent in his dark eyes.

A word, a slight indication on her part…

She had to move, put some distance between them, and the breath hitched in her throat as she pushed her hands against his chest, using leverage to widen the space.

Wolfe caught the indecision, the momentary fear…and something else. Innocent curiosity?

Curiosity, perhaps…but innocence?

He allowed her to shift to arm's length, shaping her slender frame as he skimmed his hands to cup her shoulders, aware if he released her she'd scuttle beneath the bedcovers.

'Do you want to talk about whatever pitched you into that particular hell?'

Heartfelt confidences in the depth of night, only to be regretted in the light of day?

'No.' Any rehashing would only keep the scene alive in her mind, and possibly plunge her back into it within minutes of Wolfe dousing the bedside lamp. 'I'm fine.'

Sure, she was. But she desperately needed the solace of a darkened room, not to mention a physical distance between her and the dangerous man whose power to affect her was positively lethal.

For several long seconds his eyes seared hers, seconds when she felt the pulse thud at the base of her throat, and she unconsciously lifted her hand to hide it from view.

She felt raw, and incredibly vulnerable. Wanting, needing comfort, but hesitant to seek it in case the action might be misconstrued.

A faint smile curved his lips as he leant forward and brushed his mouth to her forehead. 'Try to sleep, hmm?' Without a further word he released her, then he stood to his feet and slid between the covers of his own bed. Seconds later the room plunged into darkness as he switched off the lamp.

Lara inched low, closed her eyes and endeavoured to covet sleep, forcing herself to lie still and regiment her breathing.

It didn't work, nothing worked, and she felt inordinately restless, unable to settle in any one position.

She was unaware of exchanging the darkness of night for dark dreams that appeared in seamless, kaleidoscopic confusion…her father's violent temper and Suzanne's fear; vicious slaps from her father's hand because she wasn't quick enough to obey him; her childish sobbing as she huddled into a foetal ball in a darkened room behind a locked door.

Then strong arms cradled her close, and she instinctively clung to a warm body, holding on tight as a sense of peace seeped into her soul, providing a dreamless somnolence.

Next morning Lara woke to the muted sound of the shower in the *en suite*, and it was almost eight when she checked her watch.

That was when she noticed the bedcovers were turned back on the opposite side of her bed, the imprint of a head on the pillow beside her own.

Someone had occupied her bed.

Wolfe? Of course, *Wolfe*!

Had they…? No, of course not. She'd have remembered… and have known!

Which meant… Oh, dear heaven. Snatches of remembered dreams surfaced, and her features paled as she pinned being held through what remained of the night as reality, not part of a dream.

The sound of the *en-suite* door opening held her transfixed as Wolfe emerged into the room, a white towel hitched at his hips, his dark hair wet.

A curling sensation spiralled up inside as she took in his powerful shoulders, the broad muscular chest with its light sprinkling of dark hair arrowing down past his navel. The narrow waist, lean hips and the length of his legs.

His presence dominated the room, and she lifted her head a little and met his dark gaze.

'Good morning.' His drawled greeting curled round her nerve-ends and tugged a little.

Wolfe caught the soft tinge of pink colouring her cheeks, divined the cause, and watched the fleeting emotions chase across her expressive features.

'You slept in my bed.' A statement which verged close to an accusation, and she saw one eyebrow slant in silent query.

'It bothered you?'

Her eyes darkened. '*Yes*, damn it.'

'"Slept" being the operative word,' he reminded her as he closed the distance between them.

He stood close…too close…for she could sense the soap and shampoo he'd used, the expanse of toned muscle and sinew, and the damning knowledge she'd spent a few hours curled against his naked frame.

'You'd have preferred me to employ a more intimate distraction?'

'No. *No*,' she reiterated, and caught the amusement

apparent in those dark eyes, the slight curve of his mouth as he moved in close.

'So this will have to suffice.'

He lowered his head and 'this' became a wickedly evocative kiss that took hold of her resistance and tossed it high.

It lasted long and lingered, and it was she who groaned with frustration as he lifted his head and left her aching and needy.

'Any time you change your mind…' His soft taunt brought her down to earth with a thud, and her eyes sparked dark-blue fire.

'In your dreams!'

A husky chuckle almost undid her, and he pressed a finger against her lips.

Lara barely resisted the temptation to close her teeth and bite his finger hard. Except there was a silent warning apparent that such an action would invite retribution.

'Go get dressed. Breakfast will be delivered any time soon.'

The day lay ahead, with barely enough hours in which to achieve everything Wolfe had on his agenda.

First up was the need to confer with the interior decorator at the Point Piper mansion as they fine-tuned colour schemes, light fittings and a complete refit of the kitchen to Lara's specifications. Copious notes were made and double-checked, while the interior decorator's warmth increased to an almost obsequious level.

From there Wolfe drove to Watson's Bay where they had lunch at a charming restaurant overlooking the sea, after which they headed back to the city.

Shopping was next on the agenda, and despite Lara's protest several packages and glossy carrier bags were added to a steadily increasing collection.

'No,' Wolfe declared as she prepared to change prior to leaving for Lara's. 'Tonight you're set to experience dining *in* the restaurant, not working the kitchen.'

Lara paused in gathering her working clothes together and sent him a steady look. 'Says who?'

'I do,' he drawled. 'With Tony, Shontelle and Sally's approval.'

'But not mine,' she managed reasonably, and drew forward her trainers.

'You get to check the kitchen, then join me at six-thirty.'

She kept her voice even. 'Our busiest time.'

'You're not indispensable. The staff will cope admirably.'

They would, but that wasn't the point. 'Doesn't it matter I might *want* to work tonight?'

His eyes hardened measurably. 'Accept it's not going to happen.'

'And you intend to prevent it…how?'

'In an undignified manner, if you choose to resist.'

A few conflicting scenarios presented themselves…none of which she could possibly countenance. 'You're unbelievable!'

'So, bite me.'

'Maybe I will,' Lara threatened. 'When you least expect it.'

As an exit line, it gave some satisfaction…although it diminished somewhat in the wake of his soft laughter.

Half an hour later Lara stepped into the Lexus wearing an elegant trouser-suit, stiletto heels, make-up and with her hair caught in a smooth French roll held fast with a large clip.

In her hand she carried a bag holding trainers.

It was her kitchen, she assured herself silently. Her employees, her decision. Damn it, her final night as chef.

Tomorrow her life would change…but tonight was hers, and she resolved to play it her way.

'Hi, I didn't think you were supposed to be on kitchen duty tonight.'

Lara collected her apron, wound and fixed the ties at her waist, and offered Sally a sweet smile. 'You thought wrong.'

'Uh-oh. Trouble in paradise?'

'What makes you think that?'

Sally rolled her eyes. 'You've got the *look*.'

'And that's a bad thing?'

'If it involves Wolfe, you need to ask?'

Lara began her customary check, spoke to the staff and determined everything was as it should be as the first orders began to appear.

'It's almost six-thirty,' Tony reminded her. 'Time to go hang up your apron.'

'Soon.'

However, 'soon' wasn't soon enough.

Although, to give Wolfe credit, he allowed her ten minutes' grace before he entered the kitchen, crossed to her side, placed a hand either side of her waist and lifted her over one shoulder.

'Put me down!' The words escaped in a scandalized hiss as he turned and began walking towards the swing door. 'What do you think you're doing?'

She directed a well-aimed kick, which failed to connect, and she stifled an angry groan as Wolfe kept walking.

The indignity hit home seconds later when she heard the sound of hands clapping, and she mentally cursed him all the names she could think of...and then some.

Macho fiend. Retribution was a given, the moment she got him alone.

Which wouldn't be any time soon. Perhaps that was just as well, for right now her temper was running at an all-time high.

He came to a halt, and his hands shifted as he released her down onto her feet where she stood for a few seconds, tension apparent in every muscle of her body.

For a moment the air between them was charged with electrifying tension, and her eyes glittered with veiled vengeance as they met the dark, gleaming depths above her own.

Shock tactics were called for, and without pausing to reflect on her actions she linked her hands at his nape, leant in close and took his mouth with her own, using the tip of her tongue to explore in a manner that was entirely sensual.

Then she pulled free, stepped to one side and executed a deep curtsy…to the delight of most everyone present.

Take that, she flung in silent satisfaction, unaware of the soft pink colouring her cheeks as she straightened her apron.

She felt as if she'd been tossed through a whirlwind, and she needed a few seconds to regain her equilibrium.

It was crazy…maddening.

'Perhaps you should sit down,' Wolfe suggested with a degree of indolent amusement, and she offered him a brilliant smile.

'Thank you.'

Seated, Lara made a pretense of consulting a menu she knew by heart, ordered, and accepted a flute of champagne.

'To us,' Wolfe drawled, his eyes watchful as he touched the rim of his flute to her own.

On the surface, it was a beautiful celebratory evening. The food was superb, the ambience warm and friendly as regular patrons approached at intervals to offer their congratulations, and at closing time Lara instructed a few bottles of champagne be opened for the staff.

Anecdotes were aired and shared—the occasional disaster, and the hilarious moments…

'Remember Francois?' Sally reminded her. 'The second chef Lara hired, who prepared food fit for the gods, vowed he was of French origin, yet when Lara engaged him in conversation all he could manage was basic schoolroom French with a contrived accent that bordered on the hysterical… And we discovered he was Frank from Liverpool!

'And Duschenka, the Russian girl who answered to Du…with a tendency to throw the first thing that came to her hand whenever she lost her temper. Which was often.'

'Then there was Paul, Lara's inestimable business partner,' Shontelle revealed with an expressive shudder. 'He of the

Porsche and designer suits. Great credentials and recommendations. Very skilled at cooking the books.'

'Don't forget Gregory, who dined here every Wednesday night at eight without fail,' Sally reminisced. 'Reserved the same table, ordered precisely the same entrée and main every time, and requested a cappuccino specifically containing frothed milk with coffee on the side, sans chocolate. Then suddenly he was gone, and we never did discover a reason for his absence.'

Walking away at the end of the evening was difficult. The staff, each and every one of them, had remained loyal during the tough times, especially Sally and Shontelle, who'd been with Lara since Lara's was a new untried venture.

A soft rain-shower sprinkled the windscreen as Wolfe covered the relatively short distance to their hotel, and Lara leant back against the head-rest and closed her eyes until the Lexus slid to a halt in the hotel forecourt.

'Don't ever do that again.' The words spilled out the instant Wolfe closed the door of their suite.

'What, specifically, are you referring to?'

'Oh, *please*. Let's not play verbal games.'

He dispensed with his wallet and keys, then he shrugged out of his jacket, toed off his Italian loafers and began loosening the buttons on his shirt.

Lara turned away when he undid his belt and reached for the zip fastening.

'You want to vent, go ahead.'

She resolutely refused to offer a word, and she heard the faint rustle of clothing, followed seconds later by the soft click of the door leading into the *en suite*, only to hear it reopen minutes later.

Then he was there, and his hands closed over her shoulders as he turned her round to face him.

Dark sapphire-blue eyes glittered with banked-down anger as she met his steady gaze, and her lips parted as she prepared to rail against him.

Except he didn't give her the chance, as he captured her head between his hands and closed his mouth over her own in an erotic, evocative kiss that took all of her fine anger and tamed it.

Tamed *her*, she admitted, and left her hovering on the brink of wanting more. So much more.

For a moment she almost succumbed as his lips trailed to the sensitive hollow at the base of her throat, lingered there as he teased the throbbing pulse.

A tortured whisper emerged as she sought a vestige of control, caught in a swirling vortex where emotion ruled.

Just as she thought she could stand no more, he lifted his head and gently eased her to arm's length.

'Go to bed.' He trailed the pads of his fingers down her cheek and pressed a forefinger to her lips. 'To sleep, hmm?'

She closed her eyes, then opened them again.

He could switch off so easily?

Oh, get real. The only emotion involved here was her own. She represented a convenience. Her circumstances merely a puzzle-piece that fitted life's pattern. His, but also hers.

So accept it and move forward.

Without a word she stepped past him, collected the oversize tee-shirt she wore as a sleep-shirt, and made for the *en suite*.

When she emerged the lamp adjacent to her bed provided the room's only illumination, and she switched it off as she slid beneath the covers to lie staring into the darkness.

Tomorrow...today, she corrected on the edge of sleep... was her wedding day.

CHAPTER SEVEN

MARRIAGE, whenever Lara had given thought to the possibility of her own, would have involved the usual lead up to the event itself, with the choosing of a gown, the inevitable hen party, and Suzanne sharing in the celebrations.

Tradition, however, played no part in *this* day.

There was no breakfast served in bed. A caring message from an anxious groom-to-be didn't happen, nor the appearance of a bridesmaid or three, make-up artist and hairdresser.

Instead, Lara rose early, bade Wolfe a perfunctory 'Good morning,' as he pulled on sweats, and offered, 'Coffee?'

She needed to do something, anything, to keep her mind occupied.

'Half a cup, black, no sugar.'

A few days of occupying a hotel suite should have accustomed her to Wolfe's presence. Instead, it merely accelerated her nervous tension, and she felt the familiar curling sensation in the pit of her stomach as he crossed to her side.

Would it be easier tomorrow, the day after, when she'd shared her body with his?

Sure, and piglets should sprout wings and fly!

A hollow laugh choked in her throat, and she swallowed compulsively.

He stood close…too close…and there was nothing she

could do to prevent the fine body hairs rising up in sensual recognition.

Oh, for heaven's sake...get a grip.

Wolfe drained his coffee and replaced the cup onto the servery. 'I'll head down to the gym.'

'OK.'

Her eyes flew wide as he caught hold of her chin and tilted it so she had no option but to meet his gaze.

'Don't think of bailing out.'

His voice held a tinge of silk, and for a fleeting second he caught a glimpse of shock...and something else.

'Why would I do that?' she managed reasonably.

Why, indeed? Yet there was something evident beneath the surface he couldn't quite tap into, he reflected thoughtfully as he rode the lift down to the gym.

She kissed like an angel, and he'd be fooling himself if he said he didn't want more. To taste and savour, gift her pleasure...and take his own.

During his absence Lara showered and washed her hair, shared a leisurely breakfast with Wolfe on his return, then she began preparing for the marriage ceremony.

Make-up was minimal, with a soft pink blush adding colour to her cheeks, gloss accenting her lips, and she highlighted her eyes with a light stroke of blue to match them.

Simplicity was her chosen style, and she swept the length of her hair into a smooth twist at her nape and fixed it with a pearl-studded hinged clip.

The ivory dress with its fitted lace overlay was perfect for the marriage ceremony. Scalloped lace edged the wide scooped-neckline, the short sleeves and hemline providing a delicate fragility to her slender, petite frame. Stilettos added height, and she fixed a slender gold chain at her neck, gifted to her by Suzanne.

The final touch was a delicate spray of seed pearls fixed in her hair...and she was done.

'Ready?'

She turned to see Wolfe leaning one shoulder against the *en suite* aperture, looking incredible, she had to admit, in a superbly tailored black suit, white shirt and grey silk tie.

'Yes.' She sounded calm, when inside she was a mass of nerves.

There wasn't much she could discern from his expression, and she collected a small spray of white orchids and followed him from the suite.

The brief ceremony was due to be conducted in the hotel's private lounge in the presence of Darius' lawyer, Sally and Shontelle.

Last-minute nerves were acceptable in a bride, Lara conceded as she stood at Wolfe's side while they waited for a lift to ascend to their floor.

She was fully aware of the reasons why she'd committed herself to this marriage. So why *now* did she suddenly yearn for it to be a love match instead of a convenient merger?

How many times over the past few days had she questioned if she was doing the right thing?

Too many, she admitted, aware she'd swung like a pendulum between hesitancy and reassurance.

The lift arrived, the electronic doors slid open and she preceded Wolfe inside the empty carriage to stand in silence as they were swiftly transported down to the second level.

She didn't need prompting to smile when Wolfe took hold of her hand as they reached the private lounge.

It was show time, and she intended to give the performance of her life.

The celebrant, lawyer, Sally and Shontelle were already gathered in the elegantly furnished room. Greetings were exchanged, together with formal introductions, then without further delay the celebrant suggested the bride and groom stand together adjacent to a white-linen covered table containing a votive candle, and a crystal vase containing a delicate spray of orchids.

Wolfe threaded his fingers through her own as Lara focused on the celebrant and the deep sincerity evident in the spoken words, the deep timbre of Wolfe's voice as he made his vows…and the quiet, faintly trembling sound of her own.

Her hand shook as Wolfe slid the wide diamond-studded band onto her finger, and she almost dropped the gold band as she prepared to slide it in place on his left hand.

'I now pronounce you husband and wife.'

Lara experienced a sense of unreality as the celebrant proclaimed the words, and she barely hid her surprise as Wolfe lifted her left hand to his lips, then followed the gesture by lightly brushing his mouth to her own.

His eyes, so dark and slumbrous, rendered her boneless as she signed the marriage certificate, and it took all her effort to remain standing, to smile, even laugh on occasion, as congratulations were offered by Darius' lawyer, Sally and Shontelle.

Champagne was produced, and afterwards Lara barely held back the tears as she hugged Sally, then Shontelle, when it came time to say goodbye.

'Look after her,' both girls bade Wolfe fiercely as they paused at the hotel entrance.

'You have my word.'

It didn't take long to return to their suite and change, and Lara chose dress jeans, a knit top and jacket, then slid her feet into flat shoes…aware Wolfe had exchanged a suit for tailored trousers, a collarless shirt and soft leather jacket.

Downstairs a limousine stood waiting with their bags stowed in the boot, and the chauffeur opened the rear door as Wolfe and Lara approached.

Mascot airport lay south of the city, and as soon as the obligatory customs inspection was completed they boarded a private jet stationed at the edge of the tarmac.

Luxury fittings, Lara noticed, with the interior resembling a private lounge, with wide deep-cushioned leather recliner chairs, a work station and a personal attendant whose greeting held familiar warmth.

Did her duties include joining the mile-high club with the boss?

'No,' Wolfe drawled close to her ear as he ushered her into a seat. 'Although I'm not averse to testing the theory with my wife.'

Colour drained from her cheeks, to be rapidly replaced by twin tinges of pink. 'I don't think so.'

Musing humour gleamed in those dark eyes, and his mouth curved into a teasing smile. 'It's a long flight.' He brushed his lips to her temple. 'Buckle up. We're about to move out towards the runway.'

Show time?

If Wolfe was intent on playing a part, then so would she, and she offered him a stunning smile. 'Perhaps you should do the same…darling.'

A tad overkilled, but what did she have to lose?

No sooner had the Gulfstream jet reached the desired altitude, than Wolfe extracted his laptop and became immersed in work.

Given differing time zones, the wheels of world business never ceased, and Lara extracted a thick trade paperback Sally had gifted her, read the prologue and settled into chapter one.

The flight attendant served lunch, a delicious caesar salad followed by fresh fruit, and Lara declined coffee in favour of chilled water.

At some stage they'd need to touch down and refuel; Hawaii or LAX seemed a logical choice. Would they disembark for a stopover, or simply continue on to New York?

Lara attempted to focus on the book, the story, the characters, without much success. She felt strangely restless, with the need to stretch her legs. It was difficult to remember when she'd had so much time on her hands, unconstructive time, where she wasn't juggling several things at once with not a minute to spare.

Work and sleep had been so much the pattern of her life for endless months, it was difficult to sit and watch the world go by. Correction—the sky, and the sparse blanket of cloud beneath the jet.

The leather recliner chair was comfortable, too comfortable, and she closed the book, then leant back against the headrest.

She must have slept, for she came awake at the light touch of a hand on her shoulder, and for a moment she felt disoriented by her surroundings.

'The attendant is about to serve dinner,' Wolfe relayed quietly. 'Would you like something to drink first?'

'Chilled water,' Lara managed as she straightened in the chair.

'We're due to land on Oahu in an hour for an overnight stopover before flying on to New York tomorrow.'

The main Hawaiian island. A relaxed, laid-back lifestyle, Waikiki's sandy beach, pina coladas at sunset and the buzz of tourists, she mused when they disembarked, cleared customs, then rode a cab to downtown Waikiki.

A modern luxury hotel fronting the beach, and a magnificent suite on a high floor overlooking the wide, sweeping bay with a view towards Diamond Head.

Sparkling lights against a velvet indigo sky.

Heaven, Lara perceived, as she removed the jacket she'd worn onboard…aware Wolfe had dispensed with his own.

Had he slept during the flight? Perhaps not. He bore the invincible air of a man well used to spending long hours in the air on a regular basis.

The trick to minimizing the effects of jet lag meant adopting the current time-zone, and given it was close to midnight slipping into bed seemed a sensible option.

'You want to take the shower first, or share mine?'

Get naked with him? He had to be kidding!

Oh, get real. Tonight they'd share more than the bed. Why not view a shared shower as a tantalizing preliminary?

A fleeting thought, and one she didn't quite have the courage to implement.

Lara extracted nightwear and toiletries from her bag and crossed to the *en suite*. 'I won't be long.'

She took a few seconds to admire the splendid marble tiles lining the floor and walls, the luxurious accoutrements, then she turned on the water, set the temperature dial and quickly stripped off her clothes.

Bliss, she acknowledged as she picked up the scented soap and began smoothing it over her body. The water felt good and she lifted her face, letting the warmth flow onto it.

She didn't hear the faint sound of the bathroom door closing, only the slight snick as the partitioned glass opened, and she gasped out loud as Wolfe stepped into the large cubicle.

An arm automatically crossed over her breasts while the other defended the curling hair at the apex of her thighs.

'What do you think you're doing?' she managed as he took the soap from her hand and pulled her away from the direct water spray.

'Bathing you.'

He sounded amused, and her eyes widened as he stepped behind her and began smoothing the scented bar down the length of her spine, sensitizing her skin.

Her body swayed slightly in reaction to his touch, and she had no control over the sudden clenching sensation deep inside.

Oh… The slight groan died in her throat.

She wasn't ready for this. Not here, in the shower…

Does it matter where? a tiny voice silently taunted.

Gently, with evocative slowness, he covered every inch of

her back, the curve of her bottom, then he moved his hands up and began shaping her shoulders.

Lara felt the touch of his mouth against her nape before it trailed to the sensitive hollow at the edge of her neck, lingered there, then nibbled a little using the edge of his teeth before soothing the faintly abraded skin with an open-mouthed kiss.

It would be so easy to lean back against him, to silently indicate her compliance to everything he asked of her. Yet she couldn't quite bring herself to take that step.

What was wrong with her?

All she had to do was summon the courage and act a part.

Not even act, the tiny voice taunted remorsefully.

This was *Wolfe*…the one man who possessed the power to render her mindless.

Even now her heart hammered to a quickened beat as sensation swept through her body, and she became consumed by a deep, throbbing ache so intense it felt as if she was on fire.

With infinite care he turned her round to face him and he took hold of her chin, tilting it so she had little choice but to look at him.

His tall, broad frame seemed large in the confines of the glass cubicle, and her eyes became huge dark pools as he lowered his head and captured her mouth with his own. She expected a deliberate assault on her senses, but he kept it light, cupping her head between both hands as he gently explored the soft, moist inner tissues and savoured the contours of her tongue with the edge of his own.

The temptation to lift her arms high, link her hands at his nape and lean in against him was almost impossible to resist, and she uttered an indistinct sound as he brushed her lips with his own before lifting his head.

For an infinitesimal second she felt confused and slightly bereft as he turned slightly…then he picked up the discarded soap and handed it to her.

'Your turn, hmm?'

He had to be joking, surely?

Her hesitation brought a gleam of amusement, and he simply covered her hand with his own as he began smoothing the soap over his chest.

It was hopelessly erotic as she covered toned musculature that shifted with fluid, masculine grace beneath her touch. The tight abs, hard six-pack, to the curve of his waist.

She paused momentarily when she reached his navel, then stilled, all too aware of the potent force of his arousal.

The blatant sexuality was vaguely intimidating. Each of her previous sexual encounters…the very few of them, she amended silently…had been conducted in a bed, beneath the covers, with the lights turned off. A consensual coupling evolving from a long, affectionate friendship.

Sharing a shower was a first. Hell, total nudity in the full illuminating glare of light was another first!

Could she play the seductive vamp? Touch him, explore his body with confidence? Offer herself freely without any of the hesitant insecurity and shyness playing havoc with her senses?

Wolfe's gaze narrowed fractionally as he witnessed the fast-beating pulse at the base of her throat, the faint compulsive movement as she swallowed…and he lifted their joined hands to his mouth.

Then he released her.

For a moment she could only look at him blankly, gaining nothing from his expression, and her eyes widened as he cupped her cheek and pressed the pad of his thumb to her lower lip.

'Go get dry, hmm? I'll be out in a minute.'

What did he see? Her sense of regret…remorse?

She felt a slight tinge of warmth colour her cheeks, and she turned to escape from the shower cubicle.

Within seconds she caught up a fluffy bath-towel and quickly wound it sarong-fashion round her slim curves.

Damn it, she wouldn't flee.

Instead, she dried off, completed her nightly routine, then she tended to her hair, aware Wolfe stepped out from the shower, hitched a towel round his hips and used another towel to dry off.

He'd given her some breathing space…but for how long?

Minutes, she realized, as he unceremoniously lifted her into his arms, walked into the bedroom and slid her down to stand on her feet.

She wanted this. Hadn't she fantasized about being with him? Ached in her teenaged heart, and dreamt how it might be? Even wished to be his wife?

Foolish childish imaginings she'd thought could never come to fruition.

Yet, due to a quirk of fate, she wore Wolfe's ring on her finger and bore his name.

So what are you waiting for?

Dreams were fleeting, with the inevitable waking to reality…and normality.

Except now the dream and the reality were one and the same.

'Switch off the light.'

Wolfe captured her face between his hands. 'No.'

Her face paled, and her eyes became dark. 'Please.' Dear heaven, was that her voice? It sounded husky, *begging*, and it broke off in a soundless gasp as his mouth covered her own in a kiss that stirred her heart.

He deepened the touch, taking possession in a manner that left no doubt as to how it would end, and she caught hold of his shoulders and held on, aware his hands shifted as one cupped her nape while the other slid down to her bottom and pulled her in against him.

Lara had little recollection of when she lost the towel, or Wolfe his, aware only there was nothing separating them and his erection was a hard, turgid length against her stomach.

A soundless gasp echoed in her throat as he shifted towards the bed, then in one fluid movement he removed the covers and gently eased her down onto the sheets.

For a heart-stopping moment she could only look at him as he caged her body with his own.

His eyes were dark, so dark and slumbrous…watchful, waiting for several seemingly long seconds, then he lowered his head to her breast and brushed his lips to its soft fullness, exploring in a manner that drew sensation spiralling from the depths of her womb.

He used the edge of his teeth to tease and nip a little, before fastening on one hardened peak to suckle shamelessly… Then he moved to render a similar salutation to its twin, feasting in a manner that wrought a strangled groan from her lips.

Not content, he trailed a path to her navel, explored it with the tip of his tongue, before tracing low to the soft curls shadowing her feminine core.

'Please—' *Oh, dear heaven, please don't…* Except the words remained locked in her throat as he savoured at leisure, and she cried out as he bestowed all his attention to her throbbing clitoris, stroking the highly sensitized bud with relentless dedication until she became totally lost to the exhilarating sensation coiling through her body.

All-consuming, libidinous, pagan.

Like nothing she'd experienced, and she cried out, unable to prevent the raw, primitive sound emerging from her lips.

She moved restlessly, so caught up she didn't recognize the husky voice as her own as she begged for his possession.

Except he was far from done, and she reached for his head with both hands as he thrust his tongue deep inside…unsure in the height of passion whether she held him there or attempted to pull him free.

Just when she thought she couldn't stand the sensation

another second, he lifted his head, positioned himself…and held her gaze as he effected penetration, easing his length as she stretched to accommodate him.

Her eyes became huge dark pools, and her lips parted as he gradually filled her, then he began to move and he caught the startled surprise evident.

Unbidden, her senses coalesced into one deep ache that intensified with every stroke, until she became totally lost… *his*…in a way she'd never experienced. She wound her arms round his neck and held on as he lowered his head and took possession of her mouth, absorbing the husky cries as she went to pieces in his arms.

Was it possible for a body to vibrate? To feel so totally possessed there was no room for thought of any kind?

Lara didn't want to move…wasn't sure she *could*.

Wolfe was there, still inside her, and she felt him harden as he settled his mouth into the sensitive curve at the edge of her neck.

He trailed a path across her collarbone, then travelled back to seek the sweet hollow beneath her ear.

It felt good, so good. And she turned her head a little in a quest to have his mouth cover hers. Then she gasped with surprise as he grasped hold of her waist and rolled onto his back, taking her with him, breaking his mouth from her own as he let her assume a position of control.

She instinctively arched upwards and sank back against his bent knees, taking in the magnetic expression in those dark eyes, the disruptive sensuality apparent on his compelling features, and her lips parted as he traced the contours of each breast, then paid delicate attention to each peak.

Pleasure rippled across the surface of her skin, and her upper body shook a little as he shaped her face, her collarbone, then slid down to weigh each breast in his hands.

Evocative tracery that stirred alive her tenuous emotions…

causing her to move restlessly as one hand trailed low, seeking the acutely sensitive bud…and her reaction when he found it.

She rose up as sensation shot through her lower body in waves, each more powerful than the last, as he drove her almost to the point of delirium…then he shaped her waist and took her on the ride of her life.

Afterwards he pulled her down against him and settled her head into the curve of his neck as her body trembled in the aftershock of multiple orgasms.

His fingers drifted slowly along the edge of her spine, soothing gently until she gradually quieted and her breathing returned to normal.

She slept, physically and emotionally exhausted, unaware of the man who held her, or that it was a long time before he carefully disengaged and drew her in against the curve of his body.

CHAPTER EIGHT

THEY arrived at JFK airport in New York and were met by a chauffeur whom Wolfe introduced as Mike, who greeted them as they entered the arrivals lounge, took care of their luggage and led the way to a black top-of-the-range Mercedes parked outside the terminal.

With skilled ease they were transferred from the airport into the city.

A wise move, Lara acknowledged, given New York traffic remained the nightmare she remembered from during a visit with Suzanne and Darius.

One-way streets, traffic lights on almost every corner, reduced speed limits, traffic snarls and delays.

Cosmopolitan, loud and brash vied with refined old-money and very real wealth. A city of contrasts, where business deals were made in boardrooms and deals of a dubious kind happened on the streets. Light and dark, legitimate and subversive…a city which never slept.

She didn't know where Wolfe resided, and hadn't thought to ask. Once it had been a loft in Tribeca, but that was years ago, and he'd undoubtedly moved on and up since then.

Upper East Side, Manhattan was definitely *up*, and his roomy apartment on a high floor overlooking Central Park had to be worth a small fortune, she observed as she crossed the lounge to admire the view from floor-to-ceiling glass doors.

'A guest wing is situated beyond the dining room and kitchen on the right, and the main bedroom suite is to the left.'

There was also a home office, a media room, a guest powder-room and a small utility room, Lara noted as she followed Wolfe through to a spacious main suite with panoramic views and an adjoining *en suite* comprising marble and glass with luxurious fittings, folded fluffy towels and a double vanity along one wall.

'We'll shower and change, unpack then send out for food.'

It sounded like a plan. She hadn't slept on the flight from Hawaii, and her body still needed to adjust to New York time.

'You go first. I'll begin unpacking.'

'We could share.'

She spared him a quick look, caught the faintly teasing humour curving his generous mouth, and shook her head.

'No?' He began discarding his outer clothes, and she deliberately kept her attention averted as he moved into the *en suite*.

She retained a vivid memory of the shower they'd shared…had it only been yesterday, or had it been the night before? She attempted to do the time conversion, then gave it away; 'whenever' seemed close enough.

Her body still felt sensitive from his touch, and the mere thought of what they'd shared caused sensation to spiral deep inside, heating her blood and sending her pulse-rate racing to a faster beat.

Unpack, she bade silently, then when Wolfe re-enters the bedroom collect a change of clothes and go shower.

Hadn't she spent the past week sharing a hotel suite with him? Why the sudden onset of nerves? It hardly made sense.

She was almost done when he emerged from the bathroom, and she gathered up what she needed and entered the room he'd just vacated.

Extraction fans had removed the steam, but the soap he'd

used and his cologne teased the warm air, bringing vividly alive the effect he had on her senses.

Oh, for heaven's sake! Go with the prosaic—think food, and whether the pantry and freezer were stocked sufficiently to prepare a meal. Besides, cooking would give her something to do…

Lara dressed in jeans and a sweater, caught her hair into a loose knot atop her head, added moisturizer, took a deep breath and retraced her steps to the lounge.

Wolfe stood looking out at the city skyline, seemingly intent in conversation on his mobile phone, and she took a moment to admire his tall frame, the snug fit of his jeans and the black knit sweater which hugged and emphasized his broad shoulders.

He was something else…all harnessed power, and a degree of ruthlessness apparent beneath a sophisticated façade.

Passion, he possessed it in spades, and an intimate knowledge of precisely how to please a woman. A faint shiver slithered deliciously down her spine at the mere thought. Followed almost immediately by just how many women he'd undoubtedly slept with, where *sleep* hadn't featured on the agenda.

Did he have a mistress? A variety of obliging girlfriends who had yet to discover he'd entered into marriage?

Don't go there, a tiny voice warned.

Instead, go check out the kitchen, and if nothing else compile a list of staples and whatever else is needed.

That was where Wolfe found her, engrossed in inspecting the pantry shelves.

'I've ordered in.' He crossed to where she stood, and saw the sheet of paper and pen in her hand. 'This can wait until tomorrow.'

Sure it could, but she needed to *do* something.

'Do you entertain guests here in the apartment, or do you prefer to dine out?'

'And this is important *now*?'

He sounded mildly amused, and she added something to her list. 'Yes.'

Hands closed over her shoulders and turned her to face him. 'You're as nervous as a cat on hot bricks. Why?'

Oh hell. He saw more than she wanted him to know, and she resorted to faint cynicism. 'Because I'm shy?'

'It makes a refreshing change.'

'From the women who beat a path to your door?'

His eyes gleamed with humour. 'Those too.'

'Maybe we should notify the media—*Wolfe Alexander has moved out of the singles market*.'

'I doubt it'll be necessary.'

'Because?'

'An outstanding invitation to attend a charity fundraiser tomorrow night.'

Oh my. She was being flung in at the deep end. 'How... nice. I get to do the dress-up thing and play pretend.'

'You'll manage.'

'Of course.' The facetiousness was intended, and he responded with a soft, husky laugh that was interrupted by the buzz of the in-house intercom.

Wolfe crossed the room and checked the visual screen, the delivery person's ID, then released the entry security-door. 'Our food.'

He'd ordered in Chinese. It was delicious, and she said so as they used chopsticks to taste the contents of various containers. When they were done, they gathered the empty containers together and put them in the trash.

'Coffee?'

'Hot, black and strong. I need to put in a few hours at the laptop.'

'No problem. I'll channel-surf the cable network.'

It was pleasant to relax away from his disturbing presence,

and she settled in a comfortable leather recliner chair, found a movie on-screen that captured her attention and soon became engrossed in the storyline and the actors who played their parts.

It was around midnight that Wolfe found her there, and he stood for a moment, regarding her sleeping form in repose. She looked peaceful, and for a moment he contemplated leaving her there. Except there was every chance she'd wake disoriented by her surroundings.

Not a good option.

With care, he lifted her into his arms and carried her through to the main suite.

She didn't stir as he placed her on the bed. The slip-ons came easily off her feet, but removing her jeans required some finesse...so too did her sweatshirt.

He managed without waking her, just, and he crossed round to the opposite side of the bed, discarded his own clothes and slid in beneath the covers.

Lara woke to discover she was alone in the large bed, and within seconds the flight, the apartment...all came flooding back. So too did the recollection she'd fallen asleep while viewing television.

Dressed, she recalled.

Unless she'd sleepwalked...something she'd never done in the past...there was only one person who could have transferred her from the media room to the bedroom and removed every item of clothing except her briefs.

Wolfe.

'You're awake.'

Her eyes widened as Wolfe crossed the room to her side and extended a cup of hot, aromatic coffee.

Fully dressed in dark tailored trousers, a silk tie knotted over a pale-blue cotton shirt, and an unbuttoned waistcoat, he resembled the omnipotent city businessman she knew him to be.

Impressive, vaguely forbidding, compelling.

She was at a distinct disadvantage by comparison as she took hold of the sheet and shifted into a sitting position…only to have the sheet slip from her grasp.

A frantic tug with one hand accompanied by a swift attempt at modesty with the other more or less saved the day, although she was powerless to prevent the faint tide of pink colouring her cheeks as she accepted the coffee.

'Thanks.'

Wolfe reached forward and tucked a stray lock of hair behind her ear, then he trailed his fingers along her jawline and touched a thumb to the soft centre of her lower lip.

'Tempting,' he afforded with musing indolence, and his eyes held a teasing gleam as her colour deepened a tone. 'My driver is waiting downstairs to take me into the city office. Mike will be back in an hour and available to drive you wherever you want to go. I've left a credit card, cash and Mike has instructions to get you back here by five.'

She should thank him, and she did.

'Enjoy your day.'

Mike, it appeared, had instructions of his own, and heading the list was midtown, Madison and Fifth Avenues and a host of designer boutiques.

'Something to wear tonight, I understand,' Mike elaborated with a respectful smile.

'And you intend accompanying me?'

'You object to having a companion and guide?'

Lara sent him a telling look. 'Would it make any difference if I did?'

'Awkward,' he conceded, and she wrinkled her nose at him.

'I'm unlikely to get lost, and I have a cell phone.'

'You're a young woman alone, it's several years since you last visited New York, and it would be more than my job is worth to let you out of my sight.'

She obviously wasn't going to win independence any day soon. 'OK, so we'll do the gown thing.' After all, she *had* packed light. 'I take it we're looking for the wow factor?'

'Seriously wow.'

Designer megabucks. 'Well, then, let's get started.'

The name Wolfe Alexander meant something, it appeared, for polite enquiry soon changed to obsequious attention the moment Mike presented Wolfe's card.

It took a few hours, but the result was a stunning strapless full-length gown in coral silk, and a semi-fitted elbow-length sleeved bodice with crystal beaded detail. Exquisite stiletto-heeled evening sandals were added, and Lara relinquished the glossy designer-label carrier bags into Mike's care.

'Lunch,' she insisted as they emerged onto the pavement. 'I'm famished.'

Mike steered her towards Le Cirque on Madison, where the food and presentation were faultless, and afterwards she refused any further shopping other than groceries at a food mart.

'Smile,' Lara encouraged as Mike trod the aisles at her side while she added items from her list into the trolley. 'This is fun.'

'I'll take your word for it.'

She sent him a slightly wicked grin. 'You don't *do* groceries?'

'Other than breakfast, Wolfe rarely eats at home.'

Surely he didn't dine out every night? Which inevitably raised the question…where, and with whom, and whether 'your place or mine?' featured in the equation.

So what if it had?

And why did it seem to matter so much?

Because you care…*really* care, she added. And he doesn't. At least, not in the way you want him to care.

Moving on, taking each day…and night, as it happened… was all she could do.

Lara consulted her list. 'OK, that's it. We're done.'

Together they loaded the boot, and Mike negotiated traffic, then he helped transfer everything into the apartment.

'Thanks,' Lara said with genuine gratitude as he left to collect Wolfe. 'I appreciated your company.'

'My pleasure.'

She had two hours in which to shower, dry and style her hair, dress and apply make-up. Something she could achieve in half the time.

Wolfe entered the bedroom as she was in the process of styling her hair, and she lifted her head as he shrugged off his jacket, loosened his tie, then crossed to her side.

'Hi,' Lara offered, and her eyes widened as he captured her face and took her mouth with his own in a brief, evocative kiss.

Oh my.

'I need to shower and shave.' He began unbuttoning his shirt and pulled it free from his trousers as he moved across the room, and she lifted the brush and continued styling her hair…at least, that was what she attempted to do.

Not exactly a focused task, she had to admit when she caught a glimpse of his mirrored image as he shed his clothes.

His broad-shouldered, lean-hipped frame held a masculine beauty all its own, and she banked down the deep, curling sensation threatening to overtake her body.

The vivid memory of the shower they'd shared rose up to taunt her…the feel of his hands as he'd shaped her slender curves, the touch of his mouth, the sensations he'd aroused…

Oh, for heaven's sake…get over it!

It's just sex, and to your advantage he's so good at it. So why not go with the pleasure and forget the emotional analysis?

Tonight is your debut into New York society as Wolfe's wife, a tiny voice prompted. You have to *shine*. So tend to make-up and hair, and slip into the gown. And, when you're done, remember to adopt the expected persona for *show time*.

'Beautiful,' Wolfe complimented as he shrugged into his dinner jacket, and she executed a slight mock-curtsy.

'Thank Mike, who steered me into a number of very expensive designer boutiques downtown.'

Wolfe pocketed a billfold and checked his watch. 'We need to leave.'

They took the lift down to ground level in silence. Mike was waiting in the Mercedes as they stepped out onto the pavement, and within minutes he eased the car into the stream of traffic heading downtown.

Lara's nervous tension increased as the Mercedes pulled into the entrance of a prestigious hotel, and it accelerated as she trod the red carpet leading into the foyer.

Wolfe curved an arm along the back of her waist, and she didn't need prompting to smile. This was pretend time, and it was a given that the woman on Wolfe's arm would receive attention…some of it overt, mostly discreet.

She could do this… Hadn't she schmoozed and talked the talk at numerous stellar events in Sydney with Suzanne and Darius?

Except there, she knew people. In New York, there was only Wolfe.

'If you leave me on my own,' she warned quietly, 'I'll kill you.'

His hand slid up her spine in a soothing gesture as he leant close. 'I'm almost intrigued to let you try.'

Camera flashbulbs were in abundance, capturing the society guests as they arrived, and Lara felt a sense of relief as they reached the immense area adjoining the grand ballroom.

Uniformed waiters and waitresses circled, offering champagne, orange juice and mineral water, and she declined alcohol in favour of orange juice.

Captains of industry, society doyennes, together with some of New York's finest were in attendance, together with a cast of seemingly thousands—well, at least *one* thousand, she estimated as she sipped orange juice and watched fellow guests work the room.

'Darling Wolfe.' The faintly husky, slightly accented voice oozed sensuality and belonged to a stunning brunette, who was perfection personified from the top of her head to the tips of her designer pumps…and who made no secret of wanting to eat Wolfe alive, if she could.

Maybe she had.

Not an image on which Lara particularly wanted to dwell, for it conjured up other erotically graphic visions that were best ignored.

'Stefania.' He leaned forward and brushed his lips to her flawless cheek.

'My wife, Lara,' Wolfe introduced smoothly, and Lara saw the beautiful green eyes narrow fractionally.

'I'd heard the rumour you had married, but I did not believe it.' She touched light fingers to his mouth. 'Why, *cara*, when what we had was so good?'

Lara watched as he captured her hand and gently removed it. 'We share a friendship.'

'*Friendship*, darling?'

'You were aware it could be nothing more.'

The words were kind, his tone quiet, but the sudden, fleeting glitter in those beautiful green eyes evidenced the woman's reluctance to accept them, and her mouth formed the perfect moue before she offered Lara a brilliant smile.

'You have my congratulations.'

If looks could kill, Lara would be dead on the floor.

'Why, thank you.' She could do polite charm. Anything else was unacceptable.

'Wolfe, *amigo*.'

The hearty male voice provided a welcome intrusion, and Wolfe returned the greeting with a warm acknowledgment.

'Raf.'

'I left a message with your PA.' He turned towards Lara. 'Raf del Avica. You have my congratulations. My wife had given up hope Wolfe would ever tie the knot.' His expression became polite as he acknowledged Stefania, then he offered Lara a conciliatory smile. 'Do you mind if I borrow him for a few minutes?'

What could she say? 'Not at all.'

'You wear Wolfe's ring,' Stefania uttered with quiet vehemence as soon as both men moved out of earshot. 'But you'll never have his heart.'

This conversation had all the portents of digressing into a slang-fest. Verbal dignity was the only way to go. 'You know what they say,' Lara intimated with a faint smile. 'A reformed rake makes the best husband.'

'And why is that?'

Timing was everything. 'He's had the rest and selected the best.'

A soft derisory laugh issued from Stefania's lips. 'Don't fool yourself. A man in Wolfe's position only marries in order to breed an heir and a spare.'

Lara watched as the exotic young woman turned away and drifted through the crowd.

Well, that was fun!

She let her gaze linger on Wolfe as he conversed with Raf del Avica, noting the superb cut of his dinner jacket as it moulded his shoulders.

It was crazy, for all it took was a look and the blood fizzed in her veins. Instant recognition of a magnetic force over which she had little control…cataclysmic from the first moment she'd met him, and unrelenting in the intervening years, much to her dismay, for it had coloured her perception and become the measure by which she'd regarded the few men in her life.

Men who had been equally attractive, but lacking in the special *something* that set Wolfe apart.

Sexual chemistry…pheromones. Intense sensuality.

At that moment he turned, almost as if he sensed her appraisal, and she summoned a brilliant smile as he moved to her side.

'Tell me,' she began quietly, 'how many more women can lay claim to you?'

One eyebrow slanted a little. 'Stefania?'

'We exchanged an illuminating conversation,' she enlightened in a dry voice, and saw the edge of his mouth curve with humour.

'Who won?'

'Let's just say it was a draw.'

Minutes later the ballroom doors opened and the guests began seeking their reserved seating.

Everything ran like clockwork, Lara observed, the introductory speeches smoothly professional while uniformed waiters served drinks.

It was a sell-out, despite the expensive ticket price, and there was kudos for the entertaining artists who'd waived their usual fee in order to support a very worthy cause.

Wolfe played the part of loving husband a little too well…with a light drift of his fingers over her shoulders, the press of his hand to her thigh, lifting her hand to touch his lips fleetingly to her palm.

The most outrageous was an attempt to offer her a tempting morsel of food from his fork.

If this was a game, then two could play…and she did, resting her hand on his thigh a little too long. Only to repeat the action, dangerously high, in a seemingly innocent gesture as she engaged the guest seated opposite in scintillating conversation about the endangered species in east Africa.

'I had no idea you were so knowledgeable,' Wolfe accorded, and she offered him a teasing smile.

'Why…I'm just full of surprises.'

He leant in close. 'If you move your hand any higher…'

he warned in a silky undertone, and caught the mischievous gleam in her eyes.

'Promises, *darling*?' she murmured.

'Count on it.'

'Mmm.' She traced her upper lip with the tip of her tongue. 'Delicious.' With blithe unconcern she transferred her attention to the plate holding her main course, and cut a gourmet potato into delicate portions.

What was it about a vibrantly attractive, sensual man that caused women to test their flirting skills? she posed a while later as she used her flatware with delicate ease to sample the dessert course.

The challenge? An innate need to prove they still 'had it', for whatever reason?

Maybe to some it was just a harmless game…or possibly the several flutes of champagne were to blame.

One woman at their table became quite blatant in her attempt to gain Wolfe's attention, which irked Lara more than it should have.

It didn't help when he covered her hand with his own and caressed a light pattern over the sensitive bones.

Overkill? Or was he intent on making a statement?

She told herself she didn't care, but that wasn't entirely true.

The MC introduced the entertainment, a group of musicians who came on stage, and the ballroom lights dimmed as the group went through their number.

Wolfe leant back in his chair as he watched the fleeting expressions on Lara's features, her faint smile as she applauded a popular number, and the soft laughter at the deliberate antics of one band member as the group parodied a well-known hit.

She intrigued him on several different levels. Circumspect with his credit card, according to Mike, when he'd fully expected her to spend a small fortune.

What was more, she didn't ask for a thing…and he was

willing to swear she hadn't been sexually active for some time. Unless she was a superb actress, which he seriously doubted, her previous lovers had cared more for their own pleasure than hers.

The music faded, the overhead lights flared to full strength, and the waiters began serving coffee.

The evening was almost at a close, and Lara felt a sense of relief when Wolfe used his phone to alert Mike to bring the car to the hotel entrance.

Her first social occasion as Wolfe's wife was about to conclude, and she didn't protest as he caught hold of her hand and threaded his fingers through her own, then he offered their excuses to the remaining guests at their table and rose to his feet.

The Mercedes with Mike at the wheel was waiting for them, and within minutes the powerful car eased into traffic and headed towards their Upper East Side apartment.

It was good to be able to drop the façade as they emerged from the car at the entrance to their apartment building.

'We managed that well,' Wolfe opined as they entered the lounge, and she turned towards him.

'You mean the touchy-feely thing? Stefania? The fact you're a babe magnet?' She waited a beat or two. 'Or is Stefania off-limits?'

'This is the part where we conduct a post mortem?'

She summoned a superficial smile. 'Of all your women? How long will it take?' She deliberately arched both eyebrows. 'I would like to go to bed before dawn.'

His husky laughter undid her, and without a further word she crossed the lounge and made for the bedroom.

For a brief moment she considered occupying one of the guest rooms, only to change her mind.

Instead, she'd undress, remove her make-up, don her nightshirt, slip beneath the covers on her side of the large bed...and turn her back on him.

Not exactly subtle, but he'd get the message.

Except it didn't quite work out that way—for she pretended sleep when she heard him enter the main suite, followed by the soft rustle of clothes being removed, and several minutes later she sensed him occupy the other side of the bed.

There was a faint click as the bedside lamp plunged the room into darkness…then nothing.

Silence. No movement. And soon she detected the sound of his even breathing.

He was asleep?

How could he *do* that, when she so needed to vent…?

Conducting a silent mental fight wasn't anywhere near as satisfactory as the real thing, and she plotted his downfall in several different ways before drifting to sleep.

CHAPTER NINE

LARA woke to find the bed empty, the apartment quiet, and when she checked there was a set of keys and a note propped up against the kitchen servery from Wolfe, alerting her that he'd already left for the office.

Her phone rang as she was drinking her second cup of coffee, and she picked up to discover Wolfe on the line.

'I'll be caught up with business meetings all day,' he began without preamble. 'One of which will inevitably stretch into the evening. Don't wait dinner.'

'Fine.'

'Mike will call in the next few minutes, and take you anywhere you want to go. Shopping?'

'Thanks.'

Short, polite, the necessities covered.

What had she expected?

So why did she feel disappointed?

When Mike called, she asked to meet him downstairs in ten, and she slipped her feet into comfortable shoes, caught up a jacket, shoulderbag, keys and made for the lift.

'Fifth and Madison?' Mike queried as she slid into the front seat. 'It'll be a pleasure to act as tour guide.'

She lifted both hands in a conciliatory gesture. 'OK, I get it. Wolfe's orders.'

'Instructions,' Mike corrected as he swung out into the traffic.

It was a pleasant day, and an interesting one, as they explored the different levels of the Guggenheim museum, studying the displayed art and the special exhibitions featuring major works by nineteenth- and twentieth-century artists in the Rotunda and Tower galleries.

Mike was an easy person to converse with, and it didn't seem intrusive to ask how long he'd been in Wolfe's employ.

'Five years.'

Maybe she'd ask Wolfe to fill in some of the blanks.

Meantime there were places to go, things to see, and who better to have as a companion than someone who knew the city?

He delivered her to the apartment building just before six, and she showered, changed into jeans and a knit top, then made herself an omelette with mushrooms, tomatoes, shallots and cheese. She ate it in the dining room, tidied up the kitchen, then settled herself comfortably in the media room and surfed the cable channels, viewed a movie, then switched to a comedy special.

At eleven she closed down and went to bed, unsure when Wolfe returned, only that when she woke in the morning the bed showed signs of his occupancy, but yet another note awaited her in the kitchen...followed by a call to her phone as she was eating breakfast.

'I have back-to-back meetings set up over the next few days,' Wolfe imparted when she picked up. She offered sweetly, 'I hardly noticed you weren't here.'

'In that case, I'll wake you tonight.'

His drawled response set all her nerve-ends to vibrant life.

'I'm sure you'll be too tired.'

His soft chuckle sounded husky on the line. 'Enjoy your day.'

'I shall.'

Exercise was a wonderful stress-reliever, and when Mike

called to ascertain her plans for the day she opted for a walk through Central Park.

She sensed his inaudible groan. 'You wouldn't prefer to go shopping?'

'Are you inferring you're not up to it?' she parried lightly.

'Five kilometres, no more.'

'You're on. With one condition—we get to do lunch.' She wrinkled her nose at him. 'Research.'

'For your Sydney restaurant.'

'I have a few ideas.'

'Indeed?'

Lara listed the names of some top New York restaurants.

Mike winced. 'I'll phone ahead for reservations. I can feel my waistband expanding already.'

The sun shone, there was a slight breeze and the temperature was cool.

Ideal for walking, and she said so as they headed out.

'Isn't this great?' she enthused some time later as they passed a man-made lake, and then went on to cross a graceful bridge.

There was time for a brief shower and a change of clothes before she met Mike downstairs, and they went out for lunch. The food was divine, the floral displays dazzling, the service faultless, and people-watching provided an intriguing visual diversion.

It was late afternoon when she entered the apartment, and the thought of facing another lonely evening didn't appeal. There was a charming little bistro a short walk from Wolfe's apartment, and it would be fun to sample their food.

An hour tops and she'd be home.

Early night-time New York wasn't all that different from its Sydney counterpart; the street was well-lit and there were people walking their dogs, and a few elderly men gathered together on the sidewalk conversing in voluble Italian.

The bistro was cosy, busy, and the food surprisingly good.

It was pleasant to sit and observe, to be a patron instead of working a kitchen.

It was almost nine when she re-entered the apartment, and after ten when Wolfe arrived home.

Was it her imagination, or were the lines fanning out from the corners of his eyes a little more pronounced than she'd remembered?

'Tough day?'

He removed his jacket and loosened his tie, discarded both, then he crossed to where she sat reading a magazine. Without a word, he set the magazine aside, caged her body, then he laid his mouth on her own, explored a little, and deepened the kiss with an expertise that sent her heart racing.

'That was *hello*?' Lara queried when she caught her breath, and his eyes gleamed with amusement as he scooped her into his arms and positioned her on his lap as he sank down into the chair.

Her image had taunted him throughout the day…the tilt of her mouth when she smiled; the silky feel of her skin beneath his touch; the way she felt in his arms.

He had a need for her that surprised him. Control was an integral part of who he'd become. Essential in the way he conducted business, and natural that it spilled over into his personal life.

'I can make coffee,' she offered, and caught his gleaming gaze.

'A shower, then I get to take you to bed.' But for now, it was enough just to hold her. 'You enjoyed your walk through part of Central Park?'

He was close, so close she caught the faint muskiness of his skin as it vied with the almost undetectable drift of his cologne. 'Mike told you.' It wasn't a query, merely recognized fact.

His hand shaped her breast, lingered, then his fingers

slipped the buttons free on her knit top and sought the burgeoning peak beneath the light fabric of her bra.

'So…how was *your* day?'

'Meetings, negotiations, a conference call. Invitations.'

'Social?'

'A few,' he drawled as he stood effortlessly and placed her on her feet. He bestowed a brief, hard kiss, and headed towards their bedroom.

Lara met him as he emerged from the *en suite*, and he crossed to her side, reached for the hem of her nightshirt and drew it over her head as she unhitched the towel at his hips.

Wolfe took his time, rousing her to fever pitch as his need matched her own, and she wrapped her legs round his waist and held on as he took her to the brink, then joined her in a glorious free-fall that left them slick with sensual heat.

In the lingering aftermath he trailed light fingers over her body, exploring the soft swell of her breasts, the dip of her navel, and settled low, seeking the highly sensitized clitoris and stroking it until the breath caught in her throat and she shattered, so caught up in an exquisite climax she cried out with the intensity of it.

Lunch the next day was everything Lara expected it to be, and afterwards with Mike at her side she explored the contemporary galleries, entered one of many shops displaying crafts and exclusive gifts, and made a few purchases to take back to Sydney for Sally, Shontelle and the wait staff, as well as something quirky for Tony.

Wolfe hadn't indicated he'd be late, and she took pleasure in preparing a delicious salad, *coq au vin* with gourmet vegetables, followed by crème brûlée and fresh fruit for dessert.

It was almost seven when he entered the apartment, and the blood began pulsing heavily in her veins at the sight of him.

He was something else, and she bit back the desire to go to him, wrap her arms round his neck and invite his kiss.

Instead, she took a moment to drink in his compelling facial bone-structure, the firm muscle-tone beneath olive-toned skin, strong cheekbones, piercing dark-grey eyes…and a mouth to die for.

'Hi.'

He responded in kind. 'Interesting day?'

'Great.' She watched as he dispensed with his jacket, loosened his tie and slid the buttons free from his vest. 'I made dinner. You've time to shower and change, if you want.'

'Thanks.' He collected his jacket and hooked it over one shoulder.

Lara checked the table while he was gone, then she crossed into the kitchen and began serving the meal.

Wolfe appeared as she was ready to take the food through to the dining room, and he collected the plates while she took care of the salad dish and dessert.

Attired in black dress-jeans, a white collarless shirt with the cuffs turned back over each forearm, he appeared relaxed and at ease. A different look from the impeccably tailored three-piece business suit and silk tie.

The casual style lent him a less formidable persona…not more ordinary, for a man of Wolfe's calibre would inevitably stand apart no matter what he wore.

He projected a dramatic mesh of elemental ruthlessness and devastating sexual alchemy…a dangerous combination coveted by his fellow contemporaries, and admired by women. A bottle of Chardonnay sat chilling in a crystal ice-bucket, and Wolfe filled two goblets, touched the rim of his to her own, and offered an appropriate salutation.

The salad was crisp, the dressing tangy, and the chicken with accompanying vegetables perfection.

It had been a while since she'd prepared a meal for just two people, and there was a certain satisfaction in the provision.

What was more, it was pleasant to sit opposite Wolfe and relax, sip a little wine, and watch him unwind.

His business interests were vast and varied, she knew, and he was putting in long hours to ensure everything would run smoothly following his return to Sydney.

'I had a text message from Sally,' she relayed. 'Lara's is doing well. Tony is great.' Her mouth curved into a teasing smile. 'I think there could be a mutual attraction thing going on between those two.'

Wolfe leant back in his chair. 'The Sydney interior decorator emailed an update. Everything is on target.'

Lara began gathering plates and cutlery together. 'I'll go make coffee.'

'Before you do, isn't there something you'd like to tell me?'

There was little she could gain from his expression. 'Such as?'

'Your solitary sojourn to a bistro last night.'

For a moment she just looked at him, and disbelief sparked her eyes a brilliant blue. 'You had me followed?'

'A newspaper cameraman caught you on film as you left the bistro.'

Consternation widened her eyes, and she offered a soft oath in response. 'Why would he bother?'

'Like it or not, I lead a high-profile existence, which by virtue of our marriage now includes you.'

He retrieved a copy of the morning's newspaper from his briefcase, and opened it to the appropriate page.

The photograph was quite good. The caption: 'Wealthy magnate's new wife dines alone' followed by the by-line: 'Trouble in paradise so soon?' was pure conjecture.

It was unfortunate and unfair, and she said as much.

'I agree.'

'So what happens now? Damage control?'

'Something like that.'

'Before or after you read me the riot act?'

She thought she caught a glimpse of humour in his dark eyes, but she could have been mistaken. She drew in a deep breath, then released it.

'If you wanted to eat there, all you had to do was ask.'

Logic after the event. 'You were locked in with meetings. It was a spur-of-the-moment decision. And, besides, I can take care of myself.'

'Brave words. But not entirely accurate.'

Her eyes sparked blue fire. 'We've already done this.'

'So we get to do it again. I don't want you wandering the streets alone at night.'

'Street,' she corrected. 'In the same block, a few hundred metres from the apartment. And it was hardly *night*.'

It was ridiculous. *He* was being ridiculous…and she said so.

'Tough.'

Words temporarily failed her. 'Oh…bite me!' she flung with anger.

With that, she lifted the plates and cutlery and took them through to the kitchen. If he followed her…

He didn't, which was perhaps just as well. Otherwise she might have been tempted to hit him…hard. An action that would undoubtedly have resulted in repercussions.

There were, she decided, more subtle ways of getting back at him, and she plotted ways and means as she stacked the dishwasher.

The simplicity of the chosen scheme brought a bubble of silent laughter. Wicked, slightly sinful…but, oh, so delightfully appropriate.

Although she did entertain second thoughts as she rested against him in the early pre-dawn hours after enjoying mind-blowing sex. Intimacy to which she'd surrendered with galling ease beneath his tactile and highly evocative persuasion.

Something he did extremely well, she had to admit, as he'd used the light brush of his mouth in a feather-light tracery of each and every sensitive pleasure-pulse, to bring alive emotions over which she had little or no control.

Lara woke to a mild autumn day with weak sunshine struggling for supremacy, and she showered, dressed in tailored trousers, blouse, swept her hair into a knot and anchored it with a large hinged clip. Then she shrugged on a jacket, collected her bag, keys, and took the lift down to the lobby where Mike waited to take her shopping.

Groceries, vegetables and fruit at a marketplace, with strict adherence to a carefully compiled list. When Mike delivered her to the apartment, she declined his help and gave him the rest of the day off.

Food preparation was something at which she excelled, and she took special care to ensure each dish was spectacularly presented.

At six o'clock she brushed out her hair and twisted its length together into a careless knot, then she added lipgloss, the slightest touch of perfume…and patiently awaited Wolfe's arrival, followed by momentary apprehension as he entered the dining room after a shower and change of clothes.

Lara served the starter, took her seat opposite him…and surreptitiously observed him enjoy the painstakingly prepared oysters stuffed with Camembert and a sliver of bacon.

The main course comprised a superb salmon fillet which she'd stuffed with a delicious seafood combination of flaked crab, finely sliced prawn and scallop in a bland sauce. Accompanying it were jacket potatoes stuffed with softened cooked potato, onions, bacon, and topped with delicate cream cheese and sprinkled with chives; stuffed mushrooms, and courgette filled with a mild filling, topped with grated cheese and breadcrumbs.

'I hardly dare think what you've concocted for dessert,' Wolfe drawled as she rose from the table to go fetch it from the kitchen.

Two individual-size meringues filled with whipped cream, fresh strawberries, kiwi fruit, topped with single red and green grapes and delicately diced cantaloupe.

He sank back in his chair and regarded her thoughtfully, noting the deliberately chaste expression, the generous curve of her mouth. She hadn't, however, been able to control the fast-beating pulse at the base of her throat.

A menu comprising 'stuffed' everything. It was difficult not to laugh out loud at her not-so-subtle revenge. 'I get the message.'

Lara offered him a stunning smile. 'I was sufficiently confident you would.'

She fascinated him as no other woman did. She was a contrary mix of unpredictability and independence. Not to mention possessed of a sparkling measure of anger when roused.

'You do realize it doesn't change a thing?'

She didn't pretend to misunderstand. 'Got it. For whatever reason. But I still think you're being ridiculous.'

'Tell me,' he began with amusement, 'do you intend providing a similar menu whenever we disagree?'

'Bet on it. I've enjoyed having creative fun at your expense.'

'Perhaps you should prepare yourself for more fun,' Wolfe suggested with a degree of humour. 'You have an invitation to attend a luncheon with Abigail van Heuvre.'

'How delightful,' she managed without missing a beat. 'I shall need to consult my schedule to see if I'm free.'

'I should warn…declining one of Abigail's invitations is akin to social suicide.'

'Maybe I could arrange to break a leg before…when?'

'Thursday.'

'This week?'

'Uh-huh.'

He was amused, darn him.

'It'll be a tough call.' She sent him a singularly sweet smile. 'But I'll do my best.'

'Mike will drive you.'

She wrinkled her nose at him. 'Naturally. One must arrive in style.'

'The invitation is being hand-delivered.'

'Personally.' It was a calculated guess. 'To your office, of course.'

His eyes gleamed at her supposition. 'My PA will deal with it.'

'Abigail van...*who?*...will be most disappointed.'

'I should take you to task.'

'Will that be before or after the coffee?' she queried, in volte-face.

Wolfe's husky laughter curled round her heartstrings and tugged a little.

'It would be a shame to ignore the dessert.'

CHAPTER TEN

LUNCH next day was at a French restaurant which was famed for its classic cassoulets, which Lara selected as her order, while Mike preferred the roast duck. By mutual consent they shared each dish, declined wine and passed on dessert.

The cassoulet had an interesting texture, and she savoured the taste, the aroma, and made a calculated guess at the ingredients. Something she intended to put to the test.

'Next week, it's another French restaurant,' she declared, and grinned when Mike offered an expressive eye-roll. 'Preceded, of course, by a brisk walk.'

'You're killing me.'

'Come Thursday, you're off the hook. I've been invited to lunch, and will only need you to deliver and collect me.'

'I shall savour the day.'

They had reached a state of friendly camaraderie, which made for relaxed companionship.

An invitation to lunch with Abigail van Heuvre was akin to a royal command, Lara acknowledged, and she chose and discarded one outfit for another before settling on a superbly tailored dress and matching jacket in jade silk, with the addition of elegant stilettos. Make-up was kept to a minimum with emphasis on her eyes, and she swept her hair into a

smooth knot, anchored it with a hinged clip and added a gold
necklet, matching ear-studs and bracelet.

To even think of opting out amounted to a mortal sin, and
Lara tamped down the onset of nervous tension as Mike drew
the Mercedes to a smooth halt at the kerb adjacent the chosen
restaurant entrance.

A few minutes' leeway, which had to be a plus, and she smiled
as Mike opened the rear passenger-door ready for her to alight.

'Call when you're ready to leave. Enjoy your luncheon.'

Like that was going to happen! Any minute soon she would
face eleven women she'd never met…women who numbered
among the *crème de la crème* of New York society. And,
although undoubtedly kindly intentioned, would seek to
discover precisely why Wolfe had chosen Lara Sommers as
his wife when there were several—oh, why not go for broke
and tell it how it was?—hundreds of beautiful, well-con-
nected, eminently suitable young women who would have
killed for the opportunity.

OK, smile, she adjured silently as she crossed the sidewalk
and entered the restaurant foyer… You can do this!

'Lara.' An exquisitely attired matron moved forward and
offered an air kiss. 'Abigail van Heuvre. I'm delighted to
meet you.'

'Likewise. Thank you for the invitation.'

'The girls are gathered in the lounge enjoying drinks. We'll
go through, shall we, and I'll introduce you.'

Instant recall of aligning names with faces was a learned
skill, one Lara had mastered over the years, and she accepted
a flute of champagne, conversed with apparent ease and
prepared for the inevitable questions.

Admittedly, the women were kind. They waited until the
maître d' had seated them at their table, settled them with
drinks, proffered menus, and had a waiter take their orders.

'Wolfe's marriage came as a surprise to us all.'

Lara summoned a smile...*smiling is good*...as she gave attention to the impeccably dressed woman seated to her right.

'Really?'

With perfect make-up, beautifully groomed hair, and sporting expensive jewellery—make that *very* expensive jewellery, Lara conceded—Romy had been introduced as the wife of a wealthy city industrialist.

'Why, *yes*. We'd quite given up he would ever—' She gave a delicate pause.

'Settle with one woman?' Lara posed with a degree of humour.

'I'm fascinated, absolutely *fascinated*, to hear how you both met.'

Forget twenty questions...this was the Inquisition!

'We've known each other for years.'

'Indeed?'

There was the temptation to encapsulate it all in one hit...except it would spoil their fun. And her own, for she was sufficiently familiar with the social scene and how it worked not to be anything other than mildly entertained by the modus operandi.

'I understand there's a distant family connection.' Abigail inclined her head as she sipped vintage champagne.

Given news of her marriage to Wolfe had appeared in the Sydney newspapers and the connection had been noted, there was no reason for circumspection.

'Wolfe's widowed father married my divorced mother several years ago,' Lara informed her quietly.

'I understand they were recently victims of an automobile accident. My condolences for your loss. Such a tragedy,' Abigail offered with genuine sympathy, and Lara inclined her head in silent acknowledgment.

'I understand Wolfe is relocating to Sydney to take over his father's business interests.'

What could she say? Other than, 'Yes.'

'You must find it lonely while he's caught up in the office every day.'

'Not at all. I've enjoyed visiting the museums and galleries.'

'Oh, how…interesting.'

It was amazing how much could be conveyed in those three words, and Lara merely smiled.

'I'm looking forward to joining a scheduled walk through part of Central Park.'

'Good heavens. You don't visit a gym?' A hand was pressed to a silicone-enhanced breast.

One of the other women present leant forward and offered, 'It'll be a pleasure to include you in our luncheon parties while you're in New York. Charities, fund-raising benefits. I'll arrange an introduction to my beauty therapist. She's divine, simply divine.'

Oh my. Does it appear as if I need one? 'How kind.'

'And you must visit my vendeuse…she's amazing. I'll be in touch and confirm a day and time, shall I?'

A wicked little imp prompted Lara to impart with a degree of regret, 'My afternoons are usually occupied preparing dinner.'

There was a telling few seconds' silence.

'You don't have staff?' One of the group appeared faintly scandalized at the mere thought.

'I enjoy cooking.'

'How…domesticated.'

Lara almost felt sorry for them, and endeavoured to be kind. They were simply doing what they did best…

However, the questions kept coming…carefully composed so they didn't resemble blatant inquisitiveness…and she tempered her responses while maintaining a smile.

Two hours, tops, although it went closer to three, and it was Lara who made the move to bring the luncheon to a close by indicating the need to call her driver and leave.

Expressed thanks were politely voiced, air-kisses exchanged, together with promises to 'be in touch'.

Mike, bless him, had the Mercedes waiting at the kerb when she emerged, and he opened the rear passenger-door, saw her seated, then slid behind the wheel and eased the powerful car forward.

Lara waited until they were out of sight before she leant her head back against the cushioned rest and closed her eyes.

'You'd prefer to return to the apartment?'

'Please.'

Thankfully the distance was short, and she managed a faint smile as he drew the car to a halt outside the entrance to Wolfe's apartment building.

'Might I suggest you take something for your headache?'

Perceptive of him, and she offered a rueful grin as she thanked him and made her way through to the lobby.

As soon as she entered the apartment she toed off her stilettos, caught them in one hand and padded through to the main bedroom, where she discarded the elegant silk combo, then removed her make-up and released her hair from its smooth upswept style.

Jeans and a knit top provided a vastly different look, and she went into the kitchen, took a long, cool drink of water, then decided on fettuccini with a mushroom, bacon and cream sauce, preceded by a salad and bruschetta, for their evening meal.

When Wolfe arrived she added pasta to the pan of boiling water, set bruschetta beneath the grill to crisp, and accepted the glass of wine from his hand.

'How was lunch?'

'You mean the thinly disguised interrogation?'

His eyes gleamed with humour. 'You acquitted yourself well.' It was a statement, not a question, and she executed an expressive eye-roll in response. 'Abigail is most impressed.'

'You're kidding me. She's already been in touch?'

Wolfe lowered his head and brushed his mouth to hers. '"Charming" is the descriptive she used.'

'Well, there you go.'

She couldn't think too well, as his hands curved down her back, cupped her bottom and pulled her in against him.

'Interesting.'

All thought temporarily escaped her as he trailed his lips down her throat and savoured the sweet hollow at its base.

'I thought so.'

She sensed the amusement in his voice as he sought the fast-beating pulse at the edge of her neck, and knew it was a dead giveaway.

'You're distracting me.'

'Not well enough, it appears.' He sought the soft fullness of her breast and shaped it.

Her breathing rachetted up a few notches. 'If this is seduction…'

'You mean you're unsure?'

'The—er—evidence is quite convincing.'

His soft laughter was almost her undoing.

'What do you suggest we do about it?'

She pretended to give it some consideration. 'There's fifteen minutes before dinner.'

'Not long enough for what I have in mind.'

Sensation swirled deep inside, increasing in intensity as her imagination went into overdrive. 'A rain check?'

'No.'

She let out a gasp as he scooped her into his arms, and a helpless protest escaped her lips. 'The pasta—'

He crossed to the cook-top, turned off the heat and removed the pan. 'Taken care of.'

'The grill,' she said weakly, and he closed the dial, lowered his head and took possession of her mouth in an erotic kiss.

'Anything else?'

His eyes were dark, and dilated with a depth of passion that matched her own.

She barely managed a choked negative before he strode through to the main bedroom.

It was later, much later, they shared a leisurely shower, donned towelling robes and ate freshly cooked fettuccini standing at the kitchen servery.

SoHo, with its galleries and some very chic and arty boutiques, became a fascinating discovery…especially the numerous cafés, with their trendy façades, and the various accents of a vast cosmopolitan population.

Lara inveigled Mike to explore, to pause a while, sample a coffee and absorb the sights and sounds. It also provided a break in which to regroup.

A waiter brought bottled water on request and served their coffee, paused at the sound of Lara's voice, then queried, 'Your accent…it's Australian, isn't it?'

Lara inclined her head, caught the guy's smile and turned her attention to Mike. 'I guess we should call it a day and head home.'

'You're due to attend the Lloyd-Fox party tonight.'

Prominent family, old money, Manhattan. How could she forget? Hadn't she shopped til she dropped yesterday for *the* gown? Settled on a stunning blue dress with waterfall beading and stilettos to match? The engraved invitation stated eight for eight-thirty. Black tie.

'In the name of all the saints,' a male voice declared. 'As I live and breathe…Lara Sommers.'

She turned, caught sight of the tall, lanky frame, the sandy hair and bright blue eyes…and gave a delighted, disbelieving laugh. 'Gus!'

Whereupon she was lifted out of her seat and swung in a circle before being set down onto her feet.

'*Gustav*, darling. It adds a certain panache, don't you think?' he queried with a mocking bow. 'And this—' he gestured an arm in a wide, encompassing arc '—is my place.' He caught the ring on her finger, spared Mike a hard glance, then lifted an eyebrow in quizzical query.

'Mike is a guide who's showing me the sights.' She spared Mike a laughing grin. 'Gus and I graduated from the same French cuisine establishment.'

'Ah, those halcyon days as students of fine cuisine, wine and discovery.' Gus took her hand and pressed it to his lips. '*Chérie*. Tis but a pleasant memory.' His eyes gleamed with humour. 'You were going to open your own restaurant. Did you?'

Lara filled him in, and he assumed a soulful expression as he indicated her wedding ring. 'You didn't wait for me.' He placed a dramatic hand over his heart. 'I am devastated.'

'Always the comedian.' He'd been the life and soul of the kitchen at any number of parties…but, when it came to food, he was a maestro.

'So, what are you doing now?'

'Right this minute? Drinking your fine coffee.'

'Come on back and see my kitchen.' His eyes twinkled. 'Meet my sweet but feisty lover, and watch the maestro in action.' He threw her a dark look. 'Criticize if you dare.'

She spared Mike a conciliatory smile. 'Do you mind? I won't be long.'

'Nonsense. How can you measure time when two gourmands unite in the kitchen?'

'Gus—'

'Shh. For a while we are going to have fun, you're going to laugh at my jokes, and be impressed by my élan, yes?'

'I'm in your hands,' she conceded with solemn levity.

'Don't,' he cautioned. 'Let Ana hear you say that, and she will beat me.'

His kitchen was a chef's delight, compact, but with superbly planned placements. Ana an equal delight, a petite, dark-haired Parisian with beautiful features and small, capable hands.

For an hour they reminisced, bandied the finer points of haute cuisine and laughed... It was, without doubt, a tonic to lift the spirit, and Lara was on the point of saying goodbye when Ana gave a faint cry, and it only took one glance to determine she'd cut herself rather badly. A second glance to know medical intervention and sutures were needed.

Lara caught the concern on Gus's features, Ana's pain... and made a split-second decision. 'Go to the doctor. I'll fill in until you return. *Go*,' she urged.

It was a while before she could relay the news to Mike. 'Why don't you leave, and I'll call when I need you? Or, better yet, I'll take a cab back to the apartment.'

'Call me. Make sure of it.'

To say she was run off her feet became an understatement as she sought to keep a handle on orders. Late afternoon merged into early evening, and her phone rang as Gus raced into the kitchen.

Lara gestured interpretive sign-language and took the call.

'Where in hell are you?'

Wolfe...quietly furious, from the sound of his voice.

'I was about to call Mike.'

'I already have. He's waiting for you.'

Ana, she learned, was fine, with several stitches to show for it, and there were offered apologies, grateful thanks and a generous hug before she removed an apron, caught up her bag and exited from the kitchen to find Mike standing just inside the door.

The Lloyd-Fox party. The need to shower, dress and *shine*—with the speed of light, and even then they'd be late.

It was a party; guests were often late for a party, she consoled as Mike drew in to the apartment block, and she hurriedly thanked him and almost ran through the lobby to the bank of lifts.

It seemed to take for ever for a lift to descend, and she flew out of the carriage the instant the doors slid open at Wolfe's apartment floor.

'Don't,' Lara implored, anticipating his verbal retribution. With hurried movements she began divesting her clothes en route to the bedroom, followed by a rushed, 'I'm sorry,' as she almost flew into the *en suite*, where she took the quickest shower on record, dressed, swept her hair high, added make-up then slid her feet into stilettos.

She emerged into the lounge, met his dark gaze, and faltered at their expression. 'I can explain.'

'Save it. We need to leave.'

'I'm sorry,' she reiterated as they walked out to the lifts, and knew it sounded pathetic.

'So you've already said.'

They rode the lift in silence…a silence which extended during the short drive to their hosts' home.

'Eight for eight-thirty' encompassed drinks, then dinner… something their hostess kindly relayed she'd easily postponed upon Wolfe's phone call alerting their delay.

A fact which merely accentuated Lara's remorse. Especially as it was a sit-down dinner for forty, and the delay in serving food wouldn't have thrilled the kitchen staff one little bit.

She had to hand it to Wolfe, for he played the part of attentive husband to a solicitous fault, while she managed to act the adoring wife. No one, she was willing to swear, could have picked up it was merely a façade.

Lara conversed with fellow guests, and was utterly charming. It cost her, for the effort at pretence took its toll on her emotions, and she longed for the evening to end.

The food was excellent, one superb course after another, followed by a choice of three desserts. Then, mercifully, coffee.

It was almost midnight when Wolfe extended their thanks, bid their hosts goodnight, and summoned his driver.

Performance-wise they'd acquitted themselves well, and she let her head fall back against the leather head-rest and closed her eyes as the powerful car slid into the late-night traffic.

Lara waited until they rode the lift to their apartment before offering, 'If you're going to rage at me, at least get it over with.' Her voice sounded impossibly husky and edged with something he couldn't define.

'Four hours ago I could have shaken you within an inch of your life.' His voice was a silky purr that sent shivers down the length of her spine, and her eyes sparked brilliant blue fire.

'So why didn't you?'

The lift slid to a halt at their floor, and seconds later he released the lock, followed her into the apartment and turned to face her. 'It didn't occur to you that I might be concerned for your welfare?'

'Why?' she demanded starkly. 'Mike was with me.'

'You dismissed him and assured you'd call.'

'I was about to phone when you rang.'

'Meantime I was left in doubt as to your whereabouts, you weren't responding to text messages, and there was every chance you'd decide to be independent and seek out a cab.'

She looked at him in disbelief.

'You were in SoHo, after dark and alone,' Wolfe chided with chilling softness.

She flung vehemently, 'It couldn't be much worse than Darlinghurst after dark. And I travelled that route every night!'

'The thought of which is the stuff of nightmares.'

He framed her face and took possession of her mouth in a punishing kiss that plundered at will, ravaging in its intent.

It was as if he wanted to devour and conquer... And he almost succeeded, before he lessened the pressure and conducted a leisurely tasting, soothing the sensitive tissues until the kiss became a tantalising tease that made her forget everything, except the man and his effect on her senses.

'At the moment,' he vowed huskily, 'all I want to think about is you…in my bed, under me.'

She closed her eyes against the sight of him. 'Sex.'

'That doesn't work for you?'

More than you'll ever know. Except was it too much to hope it might become *love-making*?

Two hearts beating as one.

Twin souls in perfect accord.

For now, just sex had to be enough.

And why deny him, when it meant denying herself emotional pleasure?

Lara took initial control and linked her hands together at his nape. 'What's keeping you?'

CHAPTER ELEVEN

THERE was nothing quite like the feeling of coming home, Lara mused as the Gulfstream jet lost height, and Sydney Harbour with its legendary landmarks came into view.

The Opera House, the Harbour Bridge, linking the northern shores to the city, its span stretching across sparkling blue waters where two tugs were guiding a cruise ship into port, and ferries crossing in opposing directions between the city and northern suburbs.

New York had proved an experience in more ways than one. A month of marriage to Wolfe, sharing his lifestyle… his bed.

Uppermost, the discovery that sexual intimacy was vastly different beneath Wolfe's tutelage than she'd ever imagined possible.

There was respect for his entrepreneurial skills, and his generosity to a few worthy charities. Not to mention the power he wielded in the corporate world. He could easily have entered Darius' conglomerate and coasted through the ranks on his father's coat-tails. Instead, he'd forged his own business in another country, succeeding beyond measure.

She had begun to understand his strengths, and appreciate his integrity.

Although she couldn't say she knew the emotional heart

of the man. She had his affection, and it should be sufficient to build on…with time, possibly to even the balance.

Except she craved *more*. For Wolfe to love her, as she loved him. To be the only woman in his life…*the one*…above all others.

Oh, get over yourself! a tiny voice chided. *As if that's going to happen any time soon…if ever.*

What about the axiom 'be content with what you have'…or words to that effect?

No one had it *all*.

So, get real, accept the status quo and be satisfied it was enough.

'We'll be landing soon.'

Lara turned at the sound of Wolfe's announcement, met his enigmatic expression and was unable to divine much. A winsome smile curved her mouth. 'Yes.' She refrained from saying 'home', for, although home was inevitably the place where a person was born and raised, she'd learnt home was where the heart was. And her heart belonged to Wolfe.

Could he possibly know? Or guess?

Sadly, she couldn't imagine anything worse than confiding a love and not having it returned in kind.

'It's great to be back,' she offered, and on impulse she touched her lips to his cheek…except he moved slightly and his mouth met hers, captured it and lightly swept her tongue with his own.

Wow. All her nerve-ends leapt into life as the breath caught in her throat. Then he withdrew with a degree of reluctance.

'Seatbelts,' Wolfe reminded, and reached for hers, secured it then tended to his own.

Clearing security and customs took minimum time, and a chauffeured limousine stood waiting kerb-side to transport them to Point Piper, where grounds and gardens had been landscaped to perfection, and the house…*mansion*, Lara amended as she entered the lobby…looked incredible.

'You must have engaged an army of tradesmen to bring all this together,' she said with a degree of awe as she moved from room to room.

The interior decorator had done a magnificent job. The furniture and furnishings complemented the house beautifully, and the kitchen… Words almost failed her as she ran gentle fingers over the marble-topped surfaces and checked out the appliances. The refrigerator, freezer and pantry held food staples sufficient to meet their immediate needs.

Lara turned towards Wolfe, threw her arms around his neck and kissed him.

'Thank you. It's beautiful.'

'The kitchen?' There wasn't one woman of his acquaintance who would be so rapt over such a functional workspace.

'Yes. And *you*,' she added with sparkling sincerity, aware he could easily have settled for less expensive equipment. 'For running with the best of the best.'

She opened cupboards, pulled out deep drawers and exclaimed at the cookware, utensils. Someone had done their homework, for everything matched her preferences.

'How?' she queried simply as she turned towards him.

'The interior decorator conferred with Tony and Sally.'

Of course. Who else but another chef would understand the importance of such specialized equipment?

'I don't know what to say.'

'You can thank me later.'

She threw him a gleaming look. 'Oh, I shall.'

'I think we should check out the garage.'

Lara looked at him silently, askance, then dutifully followed him through the utility rooms to the internal door leading into the three-car garage.

The black Lexus occupied one space, while a silver BMW occupied another, and her eyes widened as Wolfe dropped a set of keys into her hand.

'Yours.'

She temporarily lost the power of speech, then she laughed, wound her arms around his neck and kissed him…thoroughly. 'Thank you.'

'Let's go check out the upstairs rooms, hmm?'

Lara placed her hand in his, felt his fingers curl around her own, and at that precise moment it would have been so easy to tell him how much she cared.

Except she bit back the words, afraid to voice them.

Instead, she showed him with her mouth, the tactile touch of her hands, with such a generosity of spirit it took hold of his heart and made him wonder how he'd ever considered his life complete without her.

Together they slept, and she woke much later as he ran a bath, then carried her naked into the *en suite* to share it with him.

This, she decided with dreamy indolence as he drew her back against the cradle of his hips and began smoothing a soapy sponge over her skin, was heaven.

The touch of his lips against the sensitive curve of her neck; the magic he created as he shaped her slim curves; the sensual exploration of every hollow, every crevice. With sensuous slowness and dedication to please and be pleasured.

Her arousal…his own…and their shared earth-shattering climax.

Afterwards, towelled dry and naked, Wolfe carried her to bed and held her curved in against him as they slept.

It took a few days for life to settle into a relatively normal routine. A call to Lara's revealed the restaurant was doing well, and Lara could barely wait to go check it out and catch up with Sally, Shontelle and Tony.

The house became her first priority, and she took time to compile a comprehensive list of groceries required to fully stock the kitchen pantry and refrigerator-freezer.

Wolfe employed a daily housekeeper, Charlotte, who

answered to Charlie, and a regular groundsman, Alex, to take care of the lawns, gardens and minor maintenance.

Wolfe spent long hours in the city-office each day, taking up the reins of Darius' various business interests, and Lara took pleasure in preparing dinner each evening.

'You'll have me adding weight if you keep this up,' Wolfe teased as he sank back in his chair at the end of a meal almost a week after their return.

The idea was laughable. His frame was in perfect symmetry, aided by an early-morning workout in the downstairs home-gym.

Several invitations had arrived in the mail during their absence in New York, and there was the need to sort through them, RSVP, and duplicate their diaries. The most pressing engagement was organized to promote one of Darius' and Suzanne's favoured charities at an event to be held in a city hotel at the weekend, and Wolfe made the necessary call to confirm their acceptance.

The next day Lara drove to the Rocks and entered Lara's just after eleven.

'Hey, Lara!' Shontelle came out from behind the desk and bestowed a hug. Whereupon Tony and Sally emerged from the kitchen, and were equally enthusiastic in their greetings.

'Coffee break coming up,' Tony declared, and Sally deftly filched four cups and saucers, then tended to the making of drip-filter coffee while the others pulled out chairs and sat at a nearby table.

'How was New York?'

'Please tell me you shopped until you dropped?'

'More importantly, how is marriage?' Sally quizzed with a wicked grin as she served the coffee and took the remaining seat.

'Fine. No. And…OK,' Lara answered in order.

It was great to be back in familiar territory, among friends, and feel totally relaxed.

'And Wolfe?' Sally persisted with genuine concern.

'Busy,' she revealed, aware both Sally and Shontelle knew there was more to the quick marriage than met the eye. 'He's had to organize his own business interests in New York, and take control of his father's conglomerate. He leaves for the city early in the morning and returns late most nights.'

'Which leaves you with time on your hands,' Shontelle deduced.

'Why don't you come in around ten and leave after three?' Tony suggested. 'We could do with the extra hand, and—'

'You could keep an eye on the place,' Sally concluded.

'You're on.' She did a quick mental review of the week ahead. 'Give me a few days.' A smile curved her lips. 'But, while I'm here…where's an apron?'

Lara helped with the lunch orders, assisted in the clean-up, and then took time at Tony's insistence to check the books.

'Looking good,' she commended when she was done. 'Attendance is up, so is the profit margin. Well done!'

It was then she remembered the gifts she'd bought in New York, and she retrieved them from her bag and distributed the brightly wrapped parcels.

Hugs and voiced thanks followed, and she decided it was time to leave.

She was almost home when her mobile phone rang, and she took a call from Wolfe relaying not to wait dinner as he'd be caught up and late home.

A few days later the need for fresh fruit and vegetables, together with milk and bread, meant a visit to the nearest supermarket, and Lara made her selections, took them to the check-out, then carried the bags and stowed them in the car.

A cute top gracing a mannequin in the window of a nearby boutique caught her eye, and she took the few steps to check it out.

Lightweight cotton, with a vee-neckline and three-quarter

sleeves in varying shades of blue, it would be ideal with white tailored trousers or a tailored white skirt.

On impulse, she entered the boutique, checked out the size, tried it on then bought it.

She emerged onto the sidewalk, and had only taken two steps towards her car when she heard her name mentioned, and she glanced up with a faint smile.

'Yes?'

Standing within touching distance was a man she couldn't recollect as being anyone she knew.

Of average height, stocky in build, he looked to be in his mid-fifties. Well-dressed…a businessman.

Who?

'You don't recognize me?'

For some reason she felt instinctively wary, and unable to explain why. 'No. I'm sorry.' A slight frown creased her forehead. 'Should I?'

'It's been a long time.'

Something niggled at her memory, a wild stab in the dark that couldn't possibly bear credence…could it?

'Marc Sommers,' he enlightened, adding as if she needed the reminder, 'Your father.'

It wasn't easy to hide a feeling of stark disbelief as her mind went into overdrive, and more than twenty years fell away.

Her father? Here?

Why?

She couldn't think of one valid reason, although suspicion quickly took seed and provided a few…not one of them good.

Memories rose up to haunt her. 'We have nothing to say to each other.'

'Please,' Marc began with seeming earnestness. 'I've only recently learned of your marriage.'

Lara noted the slight signs of dissipation evident, a manner that seemed a little too smooth and practised.

Go, a silent voice urged. Just turn and walk away.

'You want me to believe you've chosen to convey your congratulations in person?'

He spread his hands wide. 'Is it so difficult for you to believe I regret the past? They were hard years, with a low-paid job and insufficient money to meet the bills.' His expression became sorrowful. 'I'm not proud of who I was way back then.'

'I remember the fights.' Some memories never died, and she wanted to rage at him for the pain he'd inflicted, both emotional and physical. Sufficiently severe for a desperate young mother to sweep up her child and flee to safety. 'Your behaviour was unforgivable.'

'I agree.' He managed to look suitably repentant. 'I can't change your perception of those early years, but I'd like to share an interest in your future.'

Suzanne would never have countenanced such an action, and something hardened around Lara's heart. 'Why *now*?' There was a need to have him spell it out.

'I didn't know where you were.'

It didn't compute. Darius Alexander headed a prominent conglomerate whose success was often featured in the financial news. A generous benefactor to charitable causes, he'd ensured a degree of media attention in the social pages over the years.

'Really? Strange how easily you've managed to make contact now.' She turned to leave, only to have him close a hand over her arm, and she threw him a telling look.

He raised both hands in the air in silent conciliation and backed away a few steps. 'I'd like us to spend some time together.'

'I don't think so.' With that she walked towards her car, disarmed the alarm, then drove, instinctively heading towards Vaucluse and the street which housed Suzanne's and Darius' home.

It was crazy, but there was a part of her that ached for a connection to the happiness Suzanne had shared with a man who'd truly adored her. Almost as if she needed to validate her own happy childhood in a house where love and affection had gradually overshadowed fear and pain.

She had a remote to open the gates, a key to enter the house, courtesy of Darius' lawyer, and she used both, stepping into the magnificent tiled lobby, closing the door behind her. Then she simply stood, embracing the familiarity of a home she'd shared until she'd completed her education and travelled abroad.

It was akin to stepping back in time as she recalled the laughter, the parties…and her mother's happiness. The friends who'd always been welcomed, and Wolfe…every young girl's fantasy hero.

Lara smiled, remembering as she walked through the rooms at ground level. There was no accumulation of dust, and undoubtedly a cleaning team had been kept on.

The kitchen, where she'd learnt to cook beneath the capable tutelage of Eva Bensimmon, inhaling the delicious aromas and begging a knowledge of herbs and spices, the poulet, the beef…and the breathtaking desserts.

If she closed her eyes, she could easily conjure up a familiar scene—Eva's accented conversation, lessons learned, and the joy of artistic creation and presentation.

The French cuisine. Italian. *Superb*.

Lara re-entered the foyer and climbed the wide, curving staircase leading to the upper floor, touching the polished bannister where she'd once slid down with a flurry of accompanying shrieks…never to do it again.

Sadness descended as she paused hesitantly in the aperture of the main suite.

Suzanne's personal things rested on the dressing-table; the counterpane on the bed looked freshly smoothed. The his-and-hers walk-in wardrobes would hold an array of clothing Suzanne would have chosen not to pack for the trip.

Lara couldn't step into the room. Knew it would be a while before she could force herself to go through her mother's possessions.

Pain rose up inside, and she turned away, mindless of the slow tears which welled in her eyes and spilled to trail a warm rivulet down each cheek.

She wasn't conscious of moving to the bedroom suite she'd occupied for many years, or how long she stood at the window looking out over the gardens to the pool, the tennis court, as she relived the memories.

It was a while before she returned downstairs, reset the alarm, locked up and slid into her car.

Early-evening traffic was heavy, and it was almost six when she arrived at Point Piper. Wolfe's Lexus was already in the garage, and she ran lightly upstairs to their suite, aware she had half an hour in which to shower and dress before they needed to leave for the city for the evening's fund-raising event.

Wolfe emerged into the bedroom with a towel hitched at his hips, and she met his searching appraisal with a quick smile and an apology.

'Anything you want to tell me?' He loosened the towel, and she caught sight of his powerful naked frame in the instant before he pulled on briefs and added tailored trousers.

Would she ever feel comfortable witnessing him in various stages of undress? All it took was one look at him, and she began to melt.

What would he do if she played the vamp, and slowly removed each item of clothing with deliberate coquetry?

Probably be amused, she decided, by her tentative efforts.

'Right now, I need to hit the shower.'

Wolfe closed the space between them, caught hold of her

chin and tilted it so she had no recourse but to meet his enigmatic gaze.

'Security monitoring the Vaucluse mansion alerted me to
your presence there late this afternoon.' He traced her jaw with
his thumb. 'Are you OK?'

'Fine,' Lara assured, aware she hadn't fooled him in the
slightest. Except there wasn't time for an in-depth confidence.

He moved in close and took possession of her mouth in a
brief, hard kiss, then he released her. 'It'll keep.'

Twenty-five minutes later she was dressed and her make-
up complete, with her hair swept high in an elegant twist.

The gown she'd chosen to wear was a deep sapphire-blue
silk chiffon creation that hugged her slender curves and flared
in skilfully sewn panels to her ankles. A diamond-and-sap-
phire pendant on a slender gold chain together with matching
earstuds and bracelet that had been Suzanne's were Lara's
only jewellery, apart from her wedding ring. Stiletto heels
completed the outfit, and she'd added the merest touch of a
delicate perfume.

Attired in a formal black evening-suit, white cotton dress-
shirt and black bow-tie, Wolfe bore an almost barbaric attraction beneath the sophisticated façade.

There was something primitive apparent, an inherent
quality of heightened sensuality, that tore the breath from her
body and left her wanting.

Did he know?

She caught the lazy gleam in his dark eyes as he closed the
distance between them, and she stood still as he brushed light
fingers down her cheek.

'We could always stay home.'

'No,' she managed steadily. 'We couldn't.'

'Shame.' His musing drawl met with mock severity.

'You'll just have to restrain yourself.' She waited a beat.
'It'll be good for you.'

He laughed, a deep, husky sound that curled round her nerve-ends and tugged a little…aware he wasn't the only one needing to exercise constraint.

Lara collected her jewelled evening-bag and turned towards the door. 'Let's go play with the beautiful people.'

Wolfe followed her from the room, and caught hold of her hand as they descended the staircase. 'Behave.'

She offered him a stunning smile. 'Of course.'

The evening's event had been organized to raise funds for disadvantaged children, and known to be one of Darius' and Suzanne's favoured charities.

Held in a luxury inner-city hotel, many of the guests included numerous high-powered business executives and their wives, the social glitterati and society mavens, Lara noted, as she mixed and mingled in the ballroom lobby at Wolfe's side.

Air-kisses were the favoured method of greeting, and there was a sense of bemusement as women, old and young, made a point of seeking Wolfe's attention.

'He's the most intriguing man,' a well-known doyenne noted quietly.

'Yes, isn't he?' Lara agreed with a stunning smile.

'You're a fortunate young woman. He's so into you.'

You think? He's just very good at presenting a façade. Words she didn't utter as she smiled and murmured something appropriate.

'Wolfe, darling,' a breathy feminine voice intruded, and Lara turned slightly to see a beautiful young female exquisitely perfect from head to toe. The designer gown, jewellery, styled blonde hair and skilfully applied make-up combined to present a flawless image.

Oh my.

'Christina.'

Pale lacquered nails rested against his jacket lapel. 'Likewise, darling.'

'Allow me to introduce my wife, Lara.' He turned towards Lara with a smile. 'Christina del Rey, the daughter of one of Darius' business associates.'

'Christina.' Polite, *nice*… She could do both.

'We'll catch up later. Perhaps meet at the casino?'

Wolfe's arm firmed along the back of Lara's waist. 'Possibly.'

Christina's smile was breathtaking…and in Lara's opinion a mite overdone.

With a precocious wave of her fingers, Christina turned and began threading her way through the assembled guests.

'You have a conquest,' Lara observed, and met Wolfe's indolent gaze.

His fingers splayed over her hip as he leant forward and brushed his lips to her temple. 'She bothers you?'

Act like a jealous wife and say yes?

'Not at all.' She offered an innocently sweet smile, and knew he wasn't fooled in the slightest.

The ballroom doors opened, and there was a general drift of guests as they were directed towards their designated tables.

There was soft background music, and waiters moved silently among the many tables as they took orders for drinks and returned to serve them.

At the announced time, there were introductory speeches, and a detailed explanation of how existing funds had been utilized to build much-needed facilities for disadvantaged children.

Wait staff circulated unobtrusively as they served the starter, after which the first item of entertainment was a fashion parade, followed by the main course. A comedian wrought amusement from the guests as he regaled interesting anecdotes during dessert.

Whereupon the charity spokesperson called for further do-nations to furnish the new facilities, and several businessmen obliged, including Wolfe, and it was something of a relief when coffee was served.

A time during the evening when guests tended to socialize with friends seated at different tables, and it was no surprise when Christina appeared at theirs and took an empty chair at Wolfe's side.

As easily as Wolfe drew Lara into the conversation, Christina subtly moved her out of it.

Oh joy. Perhaps it would be a good move to take a walk to the powder room, and she excused herself, carelessly ignoring Wolfe's probing glance as she stood to her feet.

It took a while, for it appeared several women guests had decided the lull in the evening's activities provided an excellent opportunity to freshen up.

OK, so a little cosmetic re-touching helped, together with freshly applied lipstick. A quick check ensured all was as it should be, and Lara re-entered the ballroom, pausing here and there to acknowledge long-time acquaintances as she threaded her way to her table.

Christina flanked Wolfe on one side, and there was an older man occupying Lara's chair. A business colleague? Christina's father?

Hmm; what now? All the other chairs at their table were occupied.

At that moment Wolfe lifted his head and he smiled…damn him. There was warmth apparent in those dark eyes, and a slight teasing quirk at the edge of his mouth.

'I was about to come looking for you.' He reached out a hand and drew her onto his lap. 'Darling, this is Christina's father, Benito.'

A man who immediately vacated his chair, acknowledged the introduction, pulled up a spare chair…and looked silently askance as Wolfe made no attempt to release his wife.

Lara pressed light fingers to Wolfe's cheek. 'It might be more—er—comfortable for you if I exchange your lap for a chair.' She waited a beat, then wickedly purred, 'For now.'

There was heat apparent in his eyes, and for a moment she was held captive by the slumbrous promise evident.

As if to emphasize it, Wolfe covered her lips with his own, traced her lower lip with the tip of his tongue, then grasped her waist and transferred her onto the chair...delighting in her faintly trembling mouth and the soft pink colouring her cheeks.

His, he reflected...and knew he would never condone another man's hands on her.

A deal with millions of dollars at stake ensured Benito del Rey possessed few, if any, scruples regarding his daughter's overt behaviour.

The drift of Christina's manicured hand on Wolfe's forearm, her soft, deliberately sensual laughter...it verged on deliberate overkill, and he reached out and removed her hand without a break in conversation.

The flirtatiousness didn't cease, as he'd hoped it would, and he didn't hide his irritation when Christina's hand settled on his thigh and squeezed a little in suggestive invitation.

'Let's move to the casino. They have a fabulous nightclub, and we could dance.'

Wolfe discarded subtlety and deliberately made a play of returning the blonde's hand onto the table. 'I think not.' He turned towards Benito. 'I conduct business in the boardroom.' He kept his voice cool, distant. 'You would do well to remember any—' he paused with telling emphasis '—extraneous offers don't cut it with me.' He rose to his feet, sent Christina a telling glance, then met Benito's slightly flushed features. 'I'll instruct my lawyer to take my deal off the table.'

'You can't do that,' the older man protested.

'I just have.' He reached for Lara's hand and drew her to her feet. 'Goodnight.'

Lara applauded silently as they rode the lift down to the hotel lobby. 'Wow, I'm impressed.'

'The man's a fool.'

To consider dicing with someone of Wolfe's calibre?

Without question.

The lift slid to a halt and they crossed to the concierge's desk, where Wolfe requested his car be brought to the entrance.

The Lexus whispered through the night streets as it headed east towards Point Piper, and Lara watched abstractly as bright neon signs diminished and residential apartment buildings stood like tall sentinels against an indigo sky.

It was after midnight when Wolfe garaged the car and they entered the house. While he reset the security system Lara slipped off her stilettos, then she hooked her fingers through the straps, hitched her gown a little and ran lightly up the stairs.

Bed looked good, and she crossed to the dressing table, removed her jewellery, then reached for the zip-fastening on her gown.

Wolfe stepped behind her and completed the task, and the silk chiffon slid to the carpet in a heap, revealing thong briefs as her only item of underwear.

She felt his hands slide beneath her arms and cup each breast, testing their weight as he gently caressed each tender peak.

Primitive awareness arrowed through her body as his lips sought the sensitive pulse at the edge of her nape, bit gently, then soothed it with an open-mouthed kiss.

Careful fingers released the pins from her hair, then slid down her body to hook beneath each slender satin strap traversing her waist and divest her of the thong.

'Not fair,' Lara murmured as he shaped her hips and trailed a hand down over her stomach to the apex of her thighs.

'How so?'

'You're wearing clothes, and I'm not.'

His warm breath teased her temple. 'Want to take care of that?'

'Mmm.' She turned round to face him, caught the gleam

of passion in those dark eyes, and the corners of her mouth curved into a mischievous smile. 'The bow-tie first, I think.'

Slow…she could do slow and teasing…and she took her sweet time undoing the bow and pulling it free. Next came the buttons on his dress shirt, one by one until she pulled the cotton fabric free from his trousers in order to tend to the final two.

His jacket followed, inch by inch, as she flattened her palms against his midriff and slowly pushed upwards until she reached his shoulders, then she stepped behind him and carefully freed the tailored jacket down both his arms.

The shirt received a similar removal, and met the stumbling block of his cufflinks, and she took a moment to admire the splendid muscles bunching at his shoulder blades, the perfect symmetry of sinew, before tending to one cufflink then taking care of the second in the pair.

Trousers…hmm. The belt first, or the zip?

Zip, she decided, and she leant in against his back and reached for the zip with tentatively seeking fingers…deliberately trailed his erection, fumbled a little, heard the slight sound of his breath hissing between his teeth…and smiled as she slowly freed the fastener.

The belt buckle took some time as she deliberated over it, and she sensed a change in his breathing as his body clenched in an effort for control.

A faint sigh escaped her lips, and she crossed round to kneel at his feet as she manoeuvered one leather shoe off, then the other, before peeling off each sock.

She ignored his clenched hands as she reached up, freed the belt buckle, then watched as the fine, tailored trousers slid to the carpet and he stepped aside from them.

His boxers came next and she tugged them down, in awe of the strength of his arousal as she leant close and traced its length with the tip of her tongue.

Lara heard his husky growl a scant second ahead of his

hands reaching for her, lifting her effortlessly up his body until her legs straddled his waist…then he lowered his head and took her mouth with his own in a deep, plundering kiss that rocked her soul.

It was all she could do to wrap her arms round his neck and hang on as he readied her for his possession…then positioned his length and plunged in to the hilt, exulting in the way her vaginal muscles stretched to accommodate him then clung to hold him there.

Wolfe moved slowly at first, withdrawing almost completely before easing in with equal slowness, until she began to beg, wanting, craving the increased tempo, the rhythm that would send her soaring high as he joined her in ecstasy.

He took her to the brink, held her there, absorbed her cries and wrapped his arms round her shuddering body as she fell apart.

Then he took her to bed and curved her into the sanctuary of his body, trailed his lips fleetingly to each cheek, her closed eyelids, then settled at the edge of her mouth, smiled a little at her languorous sigh, and waited for the moment she drifted into sleep.

Their shared passion surpassed anything he'd ever experienced, and he thanked the Deity…and Darius, for his foresight.

Wolfe slept, only to wake in darkness with the awareness Lara no longer rested at his side, and he sat up as he took in the shadows, as moonlight cast the room with dim spears of light.

He saw her then, standing at the wide expanse of shuttered glass, her slender form covered in a towelling robe and her arms wrapped across her midriff.

With ease he reached for his robe, shrugged it on and crossed to stand behind her.

'Unable to sleep?' he posed quietly as he drew her back against him.

How could she say she'd woken to stark memories that had

taken her from the bed...for to remain quiescent hadn't been an option? Or that she was still partly locked there, and remaining awake was the only solution?

'You went to the house this afternoon,' Wolfe prompted, and she leaned in, felt the light press of his lips in her hair, and turned her head so her cheek rested over his heart, allowing its steady beat to soothe her.

'I needed the reassurance of knowing the happy times Suzanne shared with Darius there.'

There had to be a reason, and he waited for her to explain...except she remained silent, unwilling to mention her father. For, once she began, she wouldn't be able to stop.

'And for that you're sad?'

'No.' She swallowed painfully. 'Just incredibly pleased for her.'

'Because?'

'Darius loved her very much.'

'It was reciprocal,' Wolfe said gently. 'You only had to see them together.'

'Yes.'

'Yet there's more.'

He couldn't know. Some of it, maybe...if Darius had thought to confide in his son. But not all of it, and there could be nothing simple in relaying Marc's sudden appearance.

'It's late. We should go get some sleep.'

'I think I can help with that.'

She caught the faint thread of amusement in his voice, and smiled. 'Sleep?' she queried as he curved an arm about her waist and led her back to bed.

'Eventually. And I get to do all the work,' he promised.

He did. With exquisite care, and a gentle loving that drew sighs from her lips as he savoured every inch of her, then, just when she thought he was done, he gifted her oral pleasure that made her want to cry from the intensity of it.

Afterwards they both slept until eight, shared a leisurely shower…then over breakfast Wolfe imparted the news he'd withheld until morning.

'I need to tie up a few details in New York.'

Lara replaced her coffee cup down onto its saucer. 'When do you leave?'

'I'm due at the airport in just under two hours.'

So soon?

She didn't want him to go…but she wouldn't ask him to stay. 'How long will you be away?'

'Including air time? No more than a week. Maybe less.'

So she'd help out at the restaurant…shop a little. Take in a movie. And maybe plan a new menu for Lara's with Tony's help.

'I'll miss you.' More than he could ever believe. She rose to her feet. 'I'll help you pack.'

Years of taking numerous flights had ensured he had packing down to a fine art, but he realized she knew it and welcomed her presence anyway.

Saying goodbye was hard…much harder than he'd imagined…and he took her mouth in a deep kiss, lifted his head then pulled her in and allowed himself a leisurely exploration that left them both wanting more.

Wolfe gently disentangled her arms from around his neck, pressed his lips to hers, then moved to the garage.

Lara watched as the Lexus reversed then headed towards the gates, and it was only when it disappeared from sight that she stepped back into the lobby and closed the door.

CHAPTER TWELVE

THE house…mansion, Lara corrected…was a stunning testament to Sydney's finest firm of interior decorators, the grounds landscaped to perfection, and shopping was the last thing on her mind.

Admit it, a tiny imp prompted. *You miss Wolfe.*

In a few more days he'd wrap everything up in New York and fly home.

Meantime, she needed to occupy herself…and what better than to visit Lara's, work the kitchen and enjoy the camaraderie for a few hours?

It would be like old times, she decided as she informed Charlie of her intention, and her mouth curved into a generous smile as she eased the BMW through the electronic gates and headed towards the Rocks.

'Great to see you,' Shontelle greeted as she entered Lara's, and they shared a quick hug, then another, as Sally caught sight of her and hurried over.

Questions, laughter, and more of the same as she headed into the kitchen.

'Hey!' Tony stopped what he was doing, grabbed her by the waist and whirled her full-circle before setting her down on her feet. 'Is this a visit, or are you here to work?'

Lara offered a wicked grin. 'Well…'

'She's bored,' Tony announced. 'Possibly misses us, and chooses to be run off her feet.' He indicated a cupboard on the far wall. 'Grab an apron.'

It was good to be back, and great to fit into a familiar routine. Within a short while it seemed as if she'd never left.

So easy to laugh at Tony's outrageous jokes, to gesture a high-five with him when Sally conveyed compliments to the chef.

The kitchen ran as smoothly as clockwork, and it was *fun*. So different from a month ago when life had looked so incredibly grim.

So much had happened, Lara mused as she dribbled fresh berries over a generous slice of pavlova. All of it good. Well, mostly, apart from a hiccup or two.

Lunch was a sumptuous focaccia filled with smoked salmon and delicious salad greens, and she took a break before beginning preparations for the evening menu.

Around nine the pace began to slacken off, and Tony took a plate, added vegetables, a superb *filet mignon* and set it in front of Lara.

'Eat.' He offered a wide grin, adding, 'Compliments of the chef.'

The *filet* melted in her mouth; the potato au gratin was superb, the asparagus spears divine.

'Hmm, you're good,' she concluded when she was done, and he executed a deep bow.

'The very reason you hired me.'

'Of course. Only the best for Lara's.'

Business had picked up, the receipts showed a marked increase, and it was pay-back time. She'd need to check with her accountant, but there was every chance she could offer a pay rise. One that was long overdue…and perhaps a bonus. In the morning, she'd make the call.

Lara stayed until closing time, bade Tony, Shontelle and

Sally goodnight, then walked the short distance to where her BMW was parked.

The air was cool, with a hint of rain…typical late-spring nighttime weather, she perceived as she eased the car out of the parking area.

She felt good. Better than good, she amended as she joined the steady flow of traffic.

Wolfe's image was there…with her every minute of the day. As to the night…sensation arrowed through her body at the mere thought of what they shared in bed and out of it.

Dear heaven, she missed him every which way there was. And more…so much more.

The question was…did he miss her?

Given the time difference between Sydney and New York, text messages and emails were their main method of communication, although Wolfe's surprise phone call early that morning…brief, of necessity, but she could recall every word…and the sound of his voice had stayed with her all day.

It was close to midnight when she turned off New South Head Road into suburban Point Piper, and a wary niggle emerged as she approached her street.

The feeling persisted when the set of headlights belonging to the car behind her took the identical turn.

Was she being tailed, or was she simply prey to an overactive imagination?

She had her mobile phone, a can of capsicum spray, a modem for the gates, another for the garage, and a superb security system guarded the house.

Minutes later she issued a sigh of relief as she turned into Wolfe's driveway…and the car behind her went on by.

She re-set the security system, took a shower, then slipped into bed, satisfied with a day well spent.

The insistent peal of the phone pulled her out of deep

sleep, and she blinked in the early grey dawn, reached auto-matically for the bedside lamp, then picked up the handset.

'Lara.' Wolfe's accented voice sounded impossibly husky, and she was willing to swear her heart began racing to a quickened beat.

'Hi.'

'That's the best you can do?' His faint drawl held a teasing quality, and she leant back against the pillow.

'Considering I've gone from sleep to wide awake within seconds? Yes.'

'You prefer a more…' his fractional pause was deliberate '…leisurely awakening?'

Instant recall of precisely *how* he initiated those early-morning happenings brought alive a superfluity of sensation in several highly erogenous pleasure zones.

'Intimacy has some advantages.'

His soft laughter curled round her nerve-ends and pulled a little. 'Only some?'

'I could be more generous in person.'

'I'll hold you to that.'

'Mmm…ditto.' There was a wealth of promise existent in her deliberate purr, and she was rewarded by the huskiness evident in his voice.

'Wonder if you'll be so brave in a few days' time.'

'Count on it.'

'You do realize I've had a hard day chairing meetings?'

'Ah,' she offered gently. 'The wheeling and dealing of big business.'

'In a few hours I get to go back to my lonely hotel suite, shower, shave, dress and go out to dinner with a few business associates.'

'My heart bleeds for you.'

'Any problems?'

The question came out of left field, and totally lacked his teasing humour.

He didn't—couldn't—know about Marc Sommers.

'Why do you ask?'

A gut feeling he couldn't shake, relating to something she wasn't telling him. And his instinct was rarely off-base.

Her past? Even further back…her childhood?

Wolfe bit down an oath as his personal assistant entered his office and silently indicated his presence was required in the boardroom. He held up his hand, signalled three minutes and he'd be there.

'No particular reason,' he assured. 'I've just been called back into a meeting. Take care, hmm?'

'You too,' Lara managed before he cut the connection.

There was no way she could go back to sleep, and she pulled on sweat pants and top, then went downstairs to the gym, completed a workout, then showered, dressed and made breakfast.

The day stretched ahead, and there was a definite need to occupy herself.

However, Lara wasn't quite so confident a few hours later when she eased the BMW onto the street, drove a few hundred metres, passed a parked car, only to notice it slip in behind her own.

Coincidence? Not if the creepy feeling stealing through her body was any indication.

Perhaps she should put it to the test, stop off at Double Bay, occupy an outside table at one of the many cafés for a latte…and check if the same car appeared on the scene.

It didn't, and she began to relax as she sipped her coffee and idly watched the people passing by. It was easy to extract a notebook and pen from her bag and begin jotting down a few menu suggestions. Something different, and perhaps a few changes in salad dishes.

Lara finished her coffee and ordered another, completely

absorbed in the task at hand. She didn't see the man observing her from a distance, didn't sense his presence as he walked towards her.

It was only when he reached a metre from her table that she looked up and noticed him.

Her eyes widened in recognition.

The chance of Marc Sommers being in the same area seemed fairly slim.

'Are we going to pretend this is an accidental meeting?'

Marc took the chair opposite without asking if she'd mind. 'I followed you here, because I need to talk to you alone.'

'There's nothing to discuss.'

'Unfortunately there is.'

'I thought I made it clear—'

'Please *listen*,' Marc intercepted forcibly. 'I've siphoned off most of my wife's inheritance. All our accounts are currently being audited, and any day soon she'll learn the truth.'

Forget the niceties, Lara determined, they'd be a waste of time. 'And you expect me to help?'

She saw his eyes narrow. 'You own a restaurant. You had to benefit from your mother's will, and—'

'I'm married to a very wealthy man,' she concluded, sickened by the avaricious gleam apparent before it was quickly masked.

'Yes.'

'Let's cut straight to the chase,' she began without preamble. 'Suzanne signed a pre-nup.' She paused deliberately. 'And I don't have access to Wolfe's investments.'

'But you could.'

Lara felt sickened by his supposition, and she extracted a note from her wallet and anchored it on the table. 'Go check out the banks,' she advised. 'They're in the money-lending business.'

'They won't touch me.'

She spared him a pitying look. 'Why am I not surprised?'

It was easy to walk away, and she did…but not far. She

prayed fervently she was wrong, and it felt as if a weight had slammed into her chest as she watched her father cross the street and get into the sedan that had begun tailing her within metres of Wolfe's home.

Their address wasn't listed, their telephone number was ex-directory, and so too were their mobile-phone numbers.

Predicting Marc's next move depended on how desperate he was, and to whom he owed money.

She needed to be among friends, and the ones she valued most were at Lara's.

As always, her appearance was genuinely welcome, and within minutes she donned an apron and got to work. The camaraderie lifted her mood, and it was good to smile, laugh a little and keep busy.

It was after nine when Tony led her to a staff table and put a plate of food before her. 'Eat.'

A delectable salad with thin slivers of prime steak was delicious, and she was almost done when Sally entered the kitchen and crossed to where Lara sat.

'There's someone asking to see you,' she said quietly. 'A man. He says he's your father.'

Lara's features paled. Marc was *here*?

She placed her cutlery carefully onto the plate. 'Has he been—?'

'Drinking? Yes.'

Oh joy. This could go any which way. 'I'll take care of his bill,' she indicated. She didn't want a public confrontation…at least, not in the restaurant. Nor did she particularly want to see him alone. 'Suggest he finishes his meal, then bring him into the office.'

It was a small room, but it offered a degree of privacy.

She couldn't finish her meal, and she merely sipped the chilled water before rising to her feet.

'Trouble?'

Tony; watchful, and slightly serious.

'I can handle it.' Hopefully.

Although several minutes later she wasn't so sure, for one look at Marc's florid features, the rather fixed look in his eyes, and she felt her heart sink.

'You know why I'm here.'

There was no point in prevaricating. 'I can't help you.'

He conducted a derogatory appraisal of her slender frame. 'You can persuade your husband to be generous.'

'I won't do that.'

His face contorted. 'Damn you. Think you're a cut above everyone else, just like your mother?'

Anger rose like a tide, and with it came the vivid memories of how Suzanne had suffered at this man's hands.

'Get out.' She rose to her feet, and didn't see him move until it was too late to deflect the blow. She only felt the pain as his palm connected with her cheek, knocking her off-balance, and she blindly reached out in an effort to steady herself, crashed into a chair and fell to the floor.

Lara scrambled backwards and instinctively lifted a protective arm against further assault as he lashed out with a foot.

His boot landed painfully against her upper arm, and he readied himself to deliver another blow…

Except it never connected, for suddenly Tony had Marc in a restraining hold, and Sally moved quickly to help Lara to her feet.

Obscenities poured from Marc's mouth as Tony tightened his grip and looked at Lara. 'Want me to call the police?'

The memories flooded back—the drunken bouts of violence, Suzanne's injuries…and her own, when Suzanne hadn't been able to shield her from Marc's wrath.

'Yes.'

For the times she and Suzanne had suffered, and for Suzanne, who had simply packed a bag, gathered Lara into her arms and fled…without laying charges.

It took a while. Marc was arrested, there were statements taken, insistence she attend Accident and Emergency for an x-ray of her arm, and it was Tony who drove her there, waited with her, then returned to the restaurant to collect her car.

'All in the line of duty,' he assured her with a friendly grin as he insisted on following her home.

It was a relief to gain solitude, and a leisurely shower helped as she sought to rationalize her father's alcoholic-fuelled behaviour.

Bed looked good, and she slid beneath the covers, pillowed her head and coveted sleep.

Minutes later the shrill peal of the phone sounded loud in the room's silence, and she reached out a hand and picked up.

'How *dare* you call the police and lay charges against Marc?' The wrath was unmistakable. 'Are you insane?' the woman continued without pause. 'I'll get a lawyer—'

'Who is this?'

'Marc's wife.'

Attempting to get a word in was akin to singlehandedly stopping the momentum of a bus!

'What are you trying to do? Ruin our lives?' The pitch of her voice rose as the tirade continued. 'Damn you! I demand you withdraw the charges!'

'No,' Lara refused calmly.

'What do you mean…*no*? You *have* to.'

'Check out the police report.' She was so icily calm it was almost frightening. 'And, while you're at it, have your lawyer check records…' She named the hospital and the time period. 'They don't paint a very pretty picture.'

'Lies. All lies. I'll sue you for defamation.'

'Think carefully before you do that,' Lara cautioned, caught the stream of invective and deemed it sensible to simply cut the connection.

It wasn't easy to dismiss the harsh words, and the temptation to call Wolfe was great, just for the reassurance in hearing his voice. But New York time meant he'd be in one of several meetings…and what could he do from the opposite side of the world?

Nothing.

Distraction helped, and for a while she watched television, aware she must have slept at some stage, for she came sharply awake from the edge of a nightmare so hauntingly real her body shook with reaction.

Remaining in bed wasn't an option, and she quickly pulled on jeans and a top, caught her hair in a ponytail, then made her way downstairs to the kitchen.

The left side of her face felt painful, and there was a sizable lump on her upper arm where Marc's boot had connected.

It could have been worse. Bruises would heal, and an assault conviction, together with an anger-management course and compulsory Alcoholics Anonymous meetings, might be the wake-up call he needed.

Sure it might, she discounted with scepticism. The only reason Marc had made his presence known was to gain whatever he could from her marriage to Wolfe. And, when she wouldn't play ball, Marc made her his target. As he had done so many years ago with Suzanne.

Except Lara was no longer a frightened child. A grown young woman, she'd succeeded in her career, survived deceit and financial hardship, and emerged with her pride and principles intact.

What was more, she was in a good place, with a man who cared for her.

Love? It was too much to ask or hope for.

Possibly in time… Meanwhile, they had passion.

Just thinking about what they shared, in bed and out of it, was enough to stir a wave of longing so acute it attacked the fragile tenure of her control.

Setting up the coffee-maker didn't seem enough, for she had a desperate need to do something constructive.

OK, so she'd cook.

Turning raw ingredients into something magical was her forte and her salvation, and she checked the contents of the refrigerator and pantry, then she extracted bowls, utensils, ingredients…and proceeded to put together a batch of cookies. A divine quiche-Lorraine followed, after which she prepared a batch of pasta sauce for the freezer.

Dawn tinged the darkness with an opalescent glow, strengthening in colour as shadows faded and shapes took form.

Breakfast comprised muesli and yoghurt, followed by coffee, and a call came through from Tony as the morning progressed.

There were a few matters Lara needed to take care of, and attending the nominated police station to provide a formal statement was one of them. A call to Darius' lawyer was another.

Grocery shopping was a must, for her cooking marathon had ensured several items needed to be replaced, and she visited the supermarket, filled a trolley, then indulged herself by selecting luxury items from an upmarket deli.

The late afternoon and evening stretched ahead, and given the choice of watching cable television, DVD's, reading or catching an early night…it was no contest.

Lara's won out, hands down, and she gathered up her bag, extracted her car keys, and drove to the Rocks.

'Can't keep you away, huh?' Shontelle teased as she entered the restaurant.

'Got it in one.'

'Are you OK? Last night—'

'Is best forgotten,' Lara declared gently. 'And I'm fine. Seriously.'

'Sure?'

'Yes.' She managed a credible smile, and sought to change the subject. 'How are the evening bookings?'

'Good. Really good,' Shontelle enthused. 'We have a family pre-wedding party, some regulars, two family birthday celebrations and a group of businessmen.'

'Busy' didn't begin to cover it, Lara conceded as the evening progressed. She handled her share of the orders with dexterity and attention to detail, working in tandem with Tony so the plates went out without too much delay.

The clientele wanted freshly cooked food, and skilled preparation ensured the kitchen delivered.

It was after ten when Tony instructed her to remove her apron, grab her bag and go home.

'Trying to get rid of me?'

'I'm unsure you should even be here after last night.'

Lara lifted both hands in a gesture of surrender. 'I'm no fragile flower,' she said with a grin, and he laughed.

'Go.'

'OK, I'm out of here.'

The drive to Point Piper was achieved in minimum time, and lights activated by a timing switch shone in welcome as she cleared the gates and garaged the car.

Now that she was home, tiredness began to descend…not exactly surprising, considering she'd only had four hours sleep the previous night.

A shower, then bed, in that order, and she covered a prodigious yawn as she stripped off her clothes.

Ten minutes later she curled up in the large bed, switched off the bedside lamp and closed her eyes.

To dream pleasant images that almost seemed real. Her head was pillowed against a familiar male chest, and strong arms held her close.

She felt secure. Safe. And she shifted slightly so that her hand rested against a hard, masculine shoulder.

A hand trailed softly down the length of her back and curved round her bottom, gently squeezed a little, then drifted up to settle at her nape.

Nice.

A faint smile curved her lips, and she sighed as the hand moved to her breast.

Hmm, this was a very pleasant dream. The power of the subconscious mind was an incredible thing, she mused, as lips brushed her temple then slid down to the edge of her mouth.

Really nice.

The hand traced a path from her breast down over her stomach, and settled at the apex of her thighs.

Too real, she decided as she came sharply awake.

There was someone in the bed with her, a very *male* someone. 'Wolfe?'

There was movement as a hand reached for the lamp, illuminating the room.

'Who else were you expecting?'

Wolfe's dark eyes gleamed with amusement as soft pink coloured her cheeks, and her mouth parted, then closed again in startled surprise.

'You weren't due back for another few days.'

He cupped her left cheek and traced the line of her jaw with his thumb, probing gently as his eyes held hers.

And it was then she became aware he knew.

As to *how*… At a guess, Tony or Sally.

'There was no need for you—'

His mouth closed over her own, savoured gently, lingered, then settled against her forehead. 'No?'

He'd made phone calls, exerted authority as her next of kin, and had the radiologist's report scanned through to him… noting the existence of childhood bone damage.

And bitterly regretted not insisting she confide in him. Her antipathy regarding her father… There had to be a reason, and he'd neglected to take her up on it.

He regarded her carefully, and she was held mesmerized by the expression in his dark eyes.

'You think I'd leave you to deal with this on your own?'

Time seemed to stand still for several long seconds, and she could only look at him in silence, incapable of saying a word as he examined the bruise on her arm.

'I'm…OK,' she managed quietly, and glimpsed the faint hardening of his gaze.

'Debatable.'

How many broken bones had Lara suffered as a child?

In all probability too many, he decided grimly.

Her father would pay, and pay dearly, Wolfe promised… he'd make sure of it.

'Abuse is never OK,' Wolfe added gently. 'Believe, I'll ensure he never gets within touching distance of you again.'

She swallowed the sudden lump in her throat.

If she'd told Wolfe about her father after the initial moment of contact, none of this might have happened.

'Thanks.' Such a simple word to convey so much. She possessed courage in most things…except the ability to lay bare her heart.

'For what, specifically?'

Wolfe had gifted her so much. Except the one thing she so desperately wanted…his love.

She had his affection, his passion. And she told herself it was enough.

'Caring.'

There was something fleeting apparent in those dark eyes she found difficult to define.

'You have that, without question. You always did.'

'Even as a teenager with a giant-sized crush?' she teased.

'At eighteen you were too young…for an affair, or marriage.'

He was right, even if she hadn't believed so at the time.

Wolfe made it easy to take the initiative, and she held fast his head, then she angled her mouth against his own, deepening the kiss in an evocative exploration that caught fire as he took control.

It became everything she needed, the touch of his hands as he shaped her body, savouring every inch of it as he drove her wild. She used the edge of her teeth where she could, and heard his husky groan in response.

With one deep, pulsing thrust he entered her, stilled, until she began to toss her head from side to side in helpless frustration... Then he moved, slowly at first, building the rhythm as she caught and matched it, taking them both to passionate heights where there was no reason, no room for any thought other than the all-consuming soul-splintering emotion.

Sexual chemistry at its zenith, Lara acknowledged as the incandescent feeling slowly began to subside, leaving in its wake a piercing sweetness.

It was bliss to lie in Wolfe's arms, to enjoy the drift of his fingers as he trailed a gentle pattern over her shoulders and down the length of her spine.

She felt boneless, and so completely *his*; everything else faded into obscurity.

There was only now, and the magical inertia that followed very good sex.

Words she wanted to say remained unsaid, for if he failed to respond in kind she'd shrivel up and die an emotional death.

Go with the positives, she reminded herself on the edge of sleep. He'd left New York ahead of schedule...

Surely that had to count for something?

CHAPTER THIRTEEN

'WE'RE going *where*?' Lara queried as she dealt with the last of their breakfast dishes—Sunday morning brunch, to be precise, for they'd risen late, stroked several laps of the pool, then showered, dressed in casual gear, and eaten out on the terrace in the early summer sunshine.

'Out on the harbour,' Wolfe relayed as he crossed round the marbled counter and wrapped his arms about her midriff.

He felt so good, *this* was so good, she conceded as she leant back against him. His lips nuzzled the sweet hollow at the edge of her neck, and she felt her senses quicken.

'If you keep doing that, we won't make it anywhere,' she managed, and he lifted his head a little.

'And that would never do.' His voice was a teasing drawl as he released her.

'Shall I assemble some food together?'

Wolfe tucked a lock of hair behind her ear. 'Already taken care of.'

'Really?'

'Uh-huh.'

'There's just the two of us?'

'And someone to handle the boat.'

The day just took a brighter turn. 'I'll grab a sweater, sunglasses, a hat and sunscreen, then we're good to go.'

'Boat' was a misnomer for the sleek cabin-cruiser moored at the end of the marina, and she said so as Wolfe led the way onboard, introduced her to the man captaining the craft, then indicated the interior.

'You've hired this for the day?' Lara queried as she admired the fittings.

'Not exactly. I bought it.'

'OK.'

'Just...*OK*?' His smile almost had her melting into a puddle at his feet.

'You want me to wax lyrical?' Lara teased, enjoying the fact she could. 'It has very nice lines.' She lifted a hand and began ticking off each finger. 'Superb fittings. Quiet engine.' Seconds later, as the cruiser reversed away from its berth, she offered, 'Moves smoothly.' Her eyes sparkled as she threw him an impish grin. 'A tad like its owner.'

Wolfe gave a husky laugh. 'You'll keep.'

'Works for me.'

She was a delight, Wolfe mused. Like fine vintage-wine.

'Let's go out on deck and take in the harbour views, hmm?'

Blue skies, a slight breeze and sunshine. The man she adored at her side...what more could she want?

There were other craft on the water, small and large, some chartered to take groups on a scheduled route.

Luxury homes hugged the landscaped rock-face as they cruised past Double Bay, Darling Point and Elizabeth Bay, towards the Royal Botanic Gardens, before heading north past Middle Head.

There was a tranquility apparent...a sense of peace Lara couldn't quite explain. Almost as if she possessed a life map, where the path ahead held clarity and purpose...and indecision and doubt were no longer relevant.

Fanciful thinking?

Perhaps.

What she shared with Wolfe was good…better than good. He brought her alive in a way she'd never expected to experience, and she was happy. In the eyes of many, she had it all, and to wish for his heart, his soul, was asking too much.

'It's becoming cool,' Wolfe said quietly as he joined her at the stern and handed her a sweatshirt. 'Put this on.'

Lara complied, then she gestured towards the foreshore. 'Sydney Harbour is one of the most picturesque I've seen,' she offered as he curved an arm over her shoulders and drew her close. 'With its many coves and bays, the city's tall buildings and expensive real-estate. The many tree- and shrub-covered promontories. It's always been *home*.'

'The country in which you've been born, and the city where you've been educated and spent your youth, will always hold a special place in your heart no matter where in the world you choose to live.'

'You don't miss New York?'

'And regret the move here? No.'

The breeze teased a few tendrils of her hair, and he tucked them behind her ear.

'I had a need to make my own mark in an industry in which my father had succeeded, and I wanted to do it unaided by nepotism or in direct competition to anything Darius had achieved.'

'He admired you for it,' Lara assured him gently. 'So did Suzanne. They were both so proud.'

Wolfe brushed his lips to her temple, then he lowered his head and took her mouth in a slow, evocative tasting that melted her bones.

'Let's go eat, shall we?'

Whoever had been responsible for packing the food hamper knew their stuff…everything to tempt the most discerning gourmand was included, together with a magnum of vintage champagne chilling in the fridge.

Fresh, crunchy bread-rolls, smoked salmon, ham off the bone, a divine pâté, and salads to die for, with a delicious glazed-fruit tart to follow.

There was a sense of magic in watching the sky lighten, then slowly tinge pale orange, change to pink, deepen in colour to rose and then purple, before gradually darkening to indigo as the cruiser reached the inner harbour.

Bright neon provided a kaleidoscope of colour on tall city buildings, and streetlights vied with illumination from homes dotted along the northern shores.

'It's been a lovely day,' Lara declared as Wolfe garaged the Lexus later. 'Thank you.' She followed him into the lobby. 'Coffee?'

'Bring it into the home office. I have something for you.' He trailed light fingers down her cheek, and felt his body stir as her mouth curved into a warm smile.

'There's nothing I need.' *Except you.*

You'll have this, Wolfe vowed silently as he moved into the large office and crossed to a wall-safe concealed behind a painting, moved tumblers to gain access, then withdrew the envelope he'd placed there only days before.

He waited until she placed the coffee down onto his desk, glimpsed her curiosity as he handed her the envelope…and watched her expression as she turned back the flap and extracted the folded sheets of paper.

Her eyes widened as she saw the attached cheque, registered its possible significance, then looked at him in growing wonder. 'How—?' For a moment she was lost for words. 'Is this what I think it is?'

'Read the explanatory letter.'

She did, and her hand shook a little as she noted the bank draft represented payment in full for the amount Paul Evans had emptied from her bank accounts, plus accrued interest.

'Should I ask how you managed this?'

'The combination of a favour and private investigation.' Sufficient influence, and a sizable fee. Neither of which she'd had at her disposal. 'The duplicate sheet requires your signature.'

'Thank you.' Heartfelt words, sincerely meant. 'Can you hand me a pen?' She didn't need to think…she signed the duplicate first, then she took the cheque, turned it over, printed the appropriate legalese, countersigned it to Wolfe, and handed it to him. 'I want you to have this.' She held up a hand as he would have spoken. 'I insist.'

'You must know I won't accept it.'

'If you don't, I'll give it to your PA to bank in your personal account.'

His gaze was startlingly direct. 'No.'

Lara's eyes glittered with sapphire brilliance. 'If you don't take that cheque,' she said with quiet vehemence, 'I'll serve you stuffed *everything* every meal for the rest of your natural life. And,' she added for good measure, 'sleep in another bed.'

'For how long?'

She picked up the first thing that came to hand…his pen…and tossed it at him. *'Years!'* Then she turned towards the door.

Except Wolfe reached it first, and she was unprepared for the humour evident in his dark eyes. 'That isn't going to happen.'

'Don't bet on it!'

In one easy movement he pulled her close and lowered his head to take possession of her mouth with consummate ease.

Her struggles didn't achieve a thing, and any attempt to bite his tongue was deftly avoided, much to her dismay, as she so badly wanted to win…a fruitless task, as she should have known. Although it didn't prevent her from trying to resist succumbing to the treacherous magic he managed to weave round her senses.

He knew where to touch, and she was powerless against his flagrant seduction. Unbidden, the blood began to sing through her veins, in tandem with each increased beat of her heart.

It wasn't fair. *He* wasn't playing fair. She didn't want to become lost and hopelessly, mindlessly, adrift in a sea of stormy emotions that allowed her to swing like a pendulum between love and angst.

When he lifted his head, she could only look at him in silence for a few seemingly long seconds, and a shaky protest emerged as he lifted a hand and traced a finger across the slightly swollen contour of her lower lip.

'Don't.' The word escaped as a begging plea, and his eyes dilated, becoming dark with passion.

'Don't…what?' Wolfe began huskily. 'Kiss you? Make love with you?'

You don't understand.

The silent helplessness of not quite having the courage to give voice to the words she so desperately wanted to say almost undid her.

She needed to move away, and he let her go, watching as she turned and walked from the room. She didn't see the thoughtful, speculative expression evident, or note the gentleness apparent as he crossed round his desk and opened up his laptop.

If it was that damn important to her, he'd accept the countersigned cheque…but on his terms.

It was late when he entered the main bedroom, and he showered, then slid beneath the bedcovers and reached for her, gathering her in against him as he teased her into wakefulness.

The gentle slide of his hands as he sought the soft, textured skin beneath her tee-shirt; the touch of his lips to her temple, the slope of her cheekbone, before settling at the edge of her mouth. The lightest tracery of her mouth with the tip of his tongue…and her tentative, unbidden response.

He kept it slow, arousing her gradually into wakefulness, taking possession of her mouth when she began to protest… and then it was too late for each of them as unleashed passion transcended rational thought, and she gave herself up to the sensual delight only he could arouse.

It was almost as if he wanted to impress his need for her, so there could be no doubt as to his feelings. Yet he said nothing in the lingering aftermath as he held her, and the touch of his lips to her temple, the drift of his fingers as they traced her spine, had meaning; she wanted the words.

Wolfe slept, and so did she for a while, then she lay wakeful and strangely restless in the early pre-dawn hours, unable to sleep.

After several long minutes she carefully slid from the bed and crossed to the wide expanse of glass overlooking the infinity pool, the surface of which shimmered a little and seemed to blend into the harbour. An optical illusion, but an interesting one.

She could still feel the imprint of Wolfe's possession, his taste a tangible entity as she'd lost herself completely in him. Something she'd sworn not to do any time soon.

Yet she was defenceless against him…and always would be, she decided with increasing sadness.

Moisture gathered at the back of her eyes at the futility of it, and she blinked rapidly in an effort to prevent the tears welling and spilling ignominiously down her cheeks.

Except she was powerless to still their flow, and a soft curse escaped from her lips as she willed them to cease.

The faint click of the lamp provided illumination, and she stood perfectly still as Wolfe moved to her side.

His hands closed over her shoulders as he turned her round to face him, and his eyes narrowed at the tell-tale streak of moisture on each cheek.

'Tears, Lara?' His hands slid to capture her face. 'You didn't shed any when the loan shark sent one of his goons to shake you down. Nor when your father assaulted you. Why now?'

She shook her head, unable to formulate the words, and he

curved fingers beneath her chin and tilted it so she had no recourse but to look at him.

'You weep because of a cheque that's rightfully yours?'

It had been the catalyst, but not the reason. 'I want you to have it.'

'Why, when I so obviously don't need it?'

'Because I owe you…so much,' she managed, and he used the pad of each thumb to dispense with the moisture staining her cheek.

'You owe me nothing,' Wolfe said gently.

Lara opened her lips to argue, only to have him use his thumb to press them closed.

'I have a suggestion. Why don't we set it aside in a trust fund for our children?'

It was a master stroke, and one which held some appeal. 'I'm OK with that.' She waited a beat. 'And my father?'

'He's due to appear in court, charged with extortion and assault.'

It was nothing less than Lara had expected. 'Has—?'

'His wife discovered his misappropriation of her inheritance? Yes. I understand she intends filing for divorce.'

'I see.'

One day she'd open up and tell him about her early childhood…but now wasn't the time.

A faint smile curved his mouth, and his eyes took on a lazy gleam. 'Do you?'

Lara searched his features, and was unsure how to answer. 'I don't know what you mean.'

'You possess enormous courage,' he accorded gently. 'Use it now.'

She wasn't capable of uttering so much as a word, and he lowered his mouth to hers, explored a little, then lifted his head fractionally and held her gaze.

It was all there, clearly evident for her to see. The passion, caring…and more. And she couldn't have looked away if her life had depended on it.

What did she have to lose? *Oh, dear heaven*…everything that mattered. But if she didn't take the chance…

'It hurts so much,' she managed at last, and wondered if he knew how she was shaking inside.

'What does?'

Oh, dear Lord. She closed her eyes in an effort to still the warm moisture welling there, and failed as one fat tear spilled and rolled slowly down her cheek.

'Loving you.' There, she'd said it. Now he'd smile, and resort to condescension in order to let her down gently.

He framed her face with both hands, and brushed the tears from her cheeks with a gentle thumb. 'Was that so difficult?'

'Damn it…yes.'

'You sweet fool. You think you're in this alone?'

A lonely seed of hope took root, and she could only look at him, incapable at that moment of saying so much as a word.

'What we share is just…great sex?' His eyes blazed with an emotion she dared not define. 'Passion?'

It was all of that, and more. So much more.

'We agreed to marriage because—'

'It was a solution at the time,' Wolfe intercepted. 'For both of us.'

Her heart ached so much, it became a tangible pain.

He brushed her lips with his own, settled at the sweet curve, then slowly traced the path of her tears.

'You are the most courageous woman I know,' he said gently. 'Generous in spirit, loyal, and possessed of a rare integrity.' A warm smile parted his mouth, and she glimpsed something in his eyes that trapped the breath in her throat. 'You light up my life.'

There wasn't a word she could say.

'Is it so impossible to believe I could love you?'

Love…*love*?

Her eyes darkened into large dilated pools. 'Would…could you repeat that?'

'I thought I had it all,' Wolfe began quietly. 'Until you came into my life and brought the sun, the moon…everything that matters.' He trailed light fingers across her collarbone, then traced the soft hollow at the base of her throat. 'You confronted me on every level. Argued, and put me firmly in my place.' He shook his head. 'So fiercely independent… I was torn between wringing your neck or taking you hard and fast until you begged for mercy.' And he had…more than once.

'You crept beneath my skin, in a way no other woman ever did.' He traced the outline of her lips, and smiled as he felt them tremble beneath his touch. 'I went to New York alone, thinking some space and distance would provide some perspective. All it proved was how much I missed you.' His lips teased her temple, then settled at a sensitive pulse beneath her ear. 'You weren't there when I reached out in the night.' His warm breath slid over the surface of her skin as he sought the edge of her mouth. 'Or in the pre-dawn hours. The apartment, which had never seemed empty or lonely before, became somewhere I didn't want to be.'

Lara opened her mouth, only to have him press her lips closed.

'All I could think of every waking minute was you. The sound of your laughter, the way you smile, and how your eyes light up at the smallest pleasure.' He eased both hands over her shoulders, and shaped her arms until he reached her hands, then he threaded his fingers through her own and lifted their joined hands to his lips. 'How you feel in my arms when we make love.'

Boneless, she registered dimly. And melting. *His.*

'My wife…a young woman I'd initially regarded as a convenient possession for whom I thought respect and affection was enough.

'How wrong could I be? You became so much a part of me. The other half of my soul.

'*You*, Lara. Only you.'

She held on to his hands, afraid if she let go she'd fall into an ignominious puddle at his feet.

The one thing she'd wished for…the only thing that mattered…was hers. Gifted willingly and without demur.

The most important gift of all. Love everlasting.

A lifetime. She'd make sure of it.

And so, she knew in her heart, would he.

* * * * *

Here's a sneak peek at
THE CEO'S CHRISTMAS PROPOSITION,
the first in USA TODAY *bestselling author*
Merline Lovelace's HOLIDAYS ABROAD *trilogy*
coming in November 2008.

American Devon McShay is about to get the Christmas
surprise of a lifetime when she meets her new client,
sexy billionaire Caleb Logan, for the very first time.

Silhouette®
Desire

Available November 2008

Her breath whistled out in a sigh of relief when he exited Customs. Devon recognized him right away from the newspaper and magazine articles her friend and partner Sabrina had looked up during her frantic prep work.

Caleb John Logan, Jr. Thirty-one. Six-two. With jet-black hair, laser-blue eyes and a linebacker's shoulders under his charcoal-gray cashmere overcoat. His jaw-dropping good looks didn't score him any points with Devon. She'd learned the hard way not to trust handsome heartbreakers like Cal Logan.

But he was a client. An important one. And she was willing to give someone who'd served a hitch in the marines before earning a B.S. from the University of Oregon, an MBA from Stanford and his first million at the ripe old age of twenty-six the benefit of the doubt.

Right up until he spotted the hot-pink pashmina, that is.

Devon knew the flash of color was more visible than the sign she held up with his name on it. So she wasn't surprised when Logan picked her out of the crowd and cut in her direction. She'd just plastered on her best businesswoman smile when he whipped an arm around her waist.

The next moment she was sprawled against his cashmere-covered chest.

"Hello, brown eyes."

Swooping down, he covered her mouth with his.

Sheer astonishment kept Devon rooted to the spot for a few seconds while her mind whirled chaotically. Her first thought was that her client had downed a few too many drinks during the long flight. Her second, that he'd mistaken the kind of escort and consulting services her company provided. Her third shoved everything else out of her head.

The man could kiss!

His mouth moved over hers with a skill that ignited sparks at a half dozen flash points throughout her body. Devon hadn't experienced that kind of spontaneous combustion in a while. A *long* while.

The sparks were still popping when she pushed off his chest, only now they fueled a flush of anger.

"Do you always greet women you don't know with a lip-lock, Mr. Logan?"

A smile crinkled the skin at the corners of his eyes. "As a matter of fact, I don't. That was from Don."

"Huh?"

"He said he owed you one from New Year's Eve two years ago and made me promise to deliver it."

She stared up at him in total incomprehension. Logan hooked a brow and attempted to prompt a nonexistent memory.

"He abandoned you at the Waldorf. Five minutes before midnight. To deliver twins."

"I don't have a clue who or what you're…"

Understanding burst like a water balloon.

"Wait a sec. Are you talking about Sabrina's old boyfriend? Your buddy, who's now an ob-gyn doc?"

It was Logan's turn to look startled. He recovered faster than Devon had, though. His smile widened into a rueful grin.

"I take it you're not Sabrina Russo."

"No, Mr. Logan, I am *not*."

* * * * *

Be sure to look for
THE CEO'S CHRISTMAS PROPOSITION
by Merline Lovelace.
Available in November 2008 wherever books are sold,
including most bookstores, supermarkets,
drugstores and discount stores.

Exclusively His

Back in his bed—and he's better than ever!

Whether you shared his bed for one night—
or five years—certain men are impossible to forget!
He might be your ex, but when you're back in his bed,
the passion is not just hot, it's scorching!

Things get tricky for sensible Veronica when
she unexpectedly meets Lucien again after one
night in Paris. And now he's determined to
seduce her back into his bed....

PUBLIC SCANDAL, PRIVATE MISTRESS
by Susan Napier
#2777

Available in November.

*Look out for more Exclusively His novels
in Harlequin Presents in 2009!*

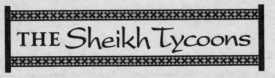

REQUEST YOUR FREE BOOKS!

2 FREE NOVELS PLUS 2 FREE GIFTS!

PASSION GUARANTEED SEDUCTION

YES! Please send me 2 FREE Harlequin Presents® novels and my 2 FREE gifts (gifts are worth about $10). After receiving them, if I don't wish to receive any more books, I can return the shipping statement marked "cancel." If I don't cancel, I will receive 6 brand-new novels every month and be billed just $4.05 per book in the U.S. or $4.74 per book in Canada, plus 25¢ shipping and handling per book and applicable taxes, if any*. That's a savings of close to 15% off the cover price! I understand that accepting the 2 free books and gifts places me under no obligation to buy anything. I can always return a shipment and cancel at any time. Even if I never buy another book, the two free books and gifts are mine to keep forever.

106 HDN ERRW 306 HDN ERRL

Name	(PLEASE PRINT)	
Address		Apt. #
City	State/Prov.	Zip/Postal Code

Signature (if under 18, a parent or guardian must sign)

Mail to the **Harlequin Reader Service:**
IN U.S.A.: P.O. Box 1867, Buffalo, NY 14240-1867
IN CANADA: P.O. Box 609, Fort Erie, Ontario L2A 5X3

Not valid to current subscribers of Harlequin Presents books.

Want to try two free books from another line?
Call 1-800-873-8635 or visit www.morefreebooks.com.

* Terms and prices subject to change without notice. N.Y. residents add applicable sales tax. Canadian residents will be charged applicable provincial taxes and GST. Offer not valid in Quebec. This offer is limited to one order per household. All orders subject to approval. Credit or debit balances in a customer's account(s) may be offset by any other outstanding balance owed by or to the customer. Please allow 4 to 6 weeks for delivery. Offer available while quantities last.

Your Privacy: Harlequin Books is committed to protecting your privacy. Our Privacy Policy is available online at www.eHarlequin.com or upon request from the Reader Service. From time to time we make our lists of customers available to reputable third parties who may have a product or service of interest to you. If you would prefer we not share your name and address, please check here. ☐

HP08R

HARLEQUIN *Presents*

EXTRA

MARRIED BY CHRISTMAS

For better or worse—she'll be his by Christmas!

As the festive season approaches, these darkly handsome Mediterranean men are looking forward to unwrapping their brand-new brides.... Whether they're living luxuriously in London or flying by private jet to their glamorous European villas, these arrogant, commanding tycoons need a wife...and they'll have one— by Christmas!

HIRED: THE ITALIAN'S CONVENIENT MISTRESS
by CAROL MARINELLI (Book #29)

THE SPANISH BILLIONAIRE'S CHRISTMAS BRIDE
by MAGGIE COX (Book #30)

CLAIMED FOR THE ITALIAN'S REVENGE
by NATALIE RIVERS (Book #31)

THE PRINCE'S ARRANGED BRIDE
by SUSAN STEPHENS (Book #32)

Happy holidays from Harlequin Presents!

Available in November.

HARLEQUIN® *Presents*

Coming Next Month

#2771 RUTHLESSLY BEDDED BY THE ITALIAN BILLIONAIRE
Emma Darcy
Ruthless

#2772 RAFAEL'S SUITABLE BRIDE Cathy Williams
Italian Husbands

#2773 MENDEZ'S MISTRESS Anne Mather
Latin Lovers

#2774 THE SHEIKH'S WAYWARD WIFE Sandra Marton
The Sheikh Tycoons

#2775 BEDDED BY THE GREEK BILLIONAIRE Kate Walker
Greek Tycoons

#2776 THE MEDITERRANEAN PRINCE'S CAPTIVE VIRGIN
Robyn Donald
The Mediterranean Princes

#2777 PUBLIC SCANDAL, PRIVATE MISTRESS Susan Napier
Exclusively His

#2778 A NIGHT WITH THE SOCIETY PLAYBOY Ally Blake
Nights of Passion

Plus, look out for the fabulous new collection *Married by Christmas* in Harlequin Presents® EXTRA:

#29 HIRED: THE ITALIAN'S CONVENIENT MISTRESS
Carol Marinelli

#30 THE SPANISH BILLIONAIRE'S CHRISTMAS BRIDE
Maggie Cox

#31 CLAIMED FOR THE ITALIAN'S REVENGE
Natalie Rivers

#32 THE PRINCE'S ARRANGED BRIDE
Susan Stephens

HPCNM1008